SIDEWINDER

RACHEL HATCH
BOOK 11

L. T. RYAN

with

BRIAN SHEA

LIQUID MIND MEDIA

For information contact:

contact@ltryan.com

http://LTRyan.com

https://www.facebook.com/JackNobleBooks

THE RACHEL HATCH SERIES

Drift

Downburst

Fever Burn

Smoke Signal

Firewalk

Whitewater

Aftershock

Whirlwind

Tsunami

Fastrope

Sidewinder

RACHEL HATCH SHORT STORIES

Fractured

Proving Ground

The Gauntlet

Join the LT Ryan reader family & receive a free copy of the Rachel Hatch story, Fractured. Click the link below to get started:

https://ltryan.com/rachel-hatch-newsletter-signup-1

Love Hatch? Noble? Maddie? Cassie? Get your very own Jack Noble merchandise today! Click the link below to find coffee mugs, t-shirts, and even signed copies of your favorite L.T. Ryan thrillers! https://ltryan. ink/EvG_

ONE

Chapter 1

MICHAEL FLATTS SLOWLY REGAINED CONSCIOUSNESS, HIS MIND GROGGY and his body aching. As his senses returned, he found himself engulfed in darkness, save for a faint, flickering light that danced along the rough-hewn walls. The musty smell of earth and stone filled his nostrils, and the air felt damp and heavy against his skin.

Blinking, he tried to clear his vision and make sense of his surroundings. The space reminded him of an old TV show he'd watched as a kid, something with a wild west theme and a mine shaft. As his eyes adjusted to the dim light, he realized he was in some sort of jail cell, the metal bars casting eerie shadows across the floor.

The cell seemed to be carved directly into the rock, the walls jagged and uneven. It was like nothing he'd ever seen before, a relic from a bygone era. The only source of light was a single bare bulb that hung from the ceiling, its weak glow barely illuminating the cramped space.

Flatts tried to move but found himself restrained. Wrists bound tightly behind his back, the rough rope bit into his skin. He struggled against his bonds, but they held fast, leaving him helpless and vulnerable.

Panic began to set in as he tried to piece together how he'd ended up in this nightmarish situation. He'd been working late at the warehouse, finishing up a shipment that had to go out first thing in the morning. He remembered locking up and heading to his car, exhausted but satisfied with a job well done. And then... nothing. His memory was a blank, a dark void that offered no clues or answers.

Mind racing, he considered the possibilities. Who would want to do this to him? He'd made his fair share of enemies over the years, back when he was running with the wrong crowd and making all the wrong choices. But that was a lifetime ago, before he'd gotten clean and turned his life around.

For over a year now, he'd been on the straight and narrow. No more drugs, no more crime. With a steady job, a loving girlfriend, and a future that finally seemed worth living for. He'd worked hard to build a new life, to leave his past behind and become a better man.

But now, as he sat in this godforsaken cell, the demons of his past seemed to be closing in on him once again. He thought of all the people he'd wronged, all the bridges he'd burned. Could one of them be behind this? Had they finally come to settle the score, to make him pay for his sins?

The questions swirled in his mind, each one more terrifying than the last. He had no idea what they wanted from him, or what they had in store. All he knew was that he had to find a way out of this hell, to get back to the life he'd fought so hard to build.

As he sat there in the darkness, his body aching and his mind reeling, Michael Flatts couldn't shake the feeling that his past had finally caught up with him, and that nothing would ever be the same again.

The door creaked open, the sound echoing through the dimly lit cell. He felt his heart race as two figures stepped inside. The first was a man he recognized all too well—Egor Novik, the ruthless leader of the Novik Crime Family. Egor's presence filled the room, his broad shoulders and thick neck straining against the collar of his expensive suit. His dark hair was slicked back, and his cold, calculating eyes fixed on him with a menacing intensity.

At Egor's side stood his top henchman, a mountain of a man known only as Volk—the Wolf. Volk's thick, muscular frame was a testament to his brutal past as a member of Russia's elite Spetsnaz forces. His bald head gleamed in the flickering light, and his thick black beard added to his intimidating appearance. Volk's reputation preceded him, a man who would do anything, no matter how violent or cruel, to carry out Egor's orders.

Flatts' heart nearly stopped when Volk dragged in a third figure, a burlap sack obscuring the face. With a brutal yank, Volk removed the hood, revealing the terrified face of Jenny, Flatts' girlfriend. Her eyes were wide with fear, tears streaming down her pale cheeks as Volk's iron grip held her in place. The sight of her in their clutches sent a wave of panic surging through Flatts, his body going rigid with horror.

Egor stepped forward, his thick Belarusian accent dripping with menace. "Well, well, well. If it isn't Michael Flatts. Or should I say, 'Burner'? That is what they called you on streets, yes?"

Burner swallowed hard, his mouth dry with fear. "Look, Egor, I'm out of the game. I've gone straight. Whatever this is about, I can't help you."

Egor chuckled, a humorless sound that sent shivers down Burner's spine. "Burner. Such a fitting name. You were always good at burning people who trusted you, weren't you? Like when you snitched to cops?"

Burner's heart sank as he realized the truth of Egor's words. He had been an informant for the police, feeding them information about the Novik family's criminal activities. It was how he had managed to escape the life, to start over with a clean slate. But now, it seemed his past had finally caught up with him.

Volk grabbed Jenny roughly, pulling her close to him. Drawing a large, wicked-looking knife from his belt, he held it against her throat. Jenny whimpered in fear, her eyes pleading with Burner to save her.

"You helped Detective Linden set up my brother, Anton," Egor said, his voice low and dangerous. "You betrayed him, betrayed family. And now, you will pay price."

Burner's mind raced as he remembered the day he had helped

Harvey Linden, a determined detective, take down Anton Novik. It had been a risky move, but one that had ultimately allowed him to escape the clutches of the crime family and start a new life. But now, as he looked into Egor's cold, merciless eyes, he realized the true cost of his betrayal.

"Please," Burner begged, his voice trembling. "Leave Jenny out of this. She has nothing to do with any of it."

Egor smiled, a cruel, twisted expression that held no warmth. "Oh, but she does. She is your weakness, your vulnerability. And we will use her to make you do what we want."

As Volk pressed the blade tighter against Jenny's throat, Burner felt a wave of despair wash over him. He had no idea what Egor wanted from him, or what he would be forced to do to keep Jenny safe.

Memories flashed through Burner's mind, vivid and painful. He remembered the day Linden had approached him, promising protection and a fresh start if he helped take down Anton Novik. Burner had been hesitant at first, but Linden's persuasive words and the chance at a new life had won him over.

Burner had risked everything, wearing a wire, gathering evidence, and testifying against Anton in court. It had been the most difficult decision of his life, but Linden's promise of a better future had given him the courage to see it through.

And for a time, it seemed that promise had been fulfilled. Anton was sent to prison, and the Novik empire crumbled. Burner had been given a new identity and the opportunity to start over. But deep down, he knew the Noviks would never forget, never forgive his betrayal.

"That was a long time ago," Burner said, his heart pounding in his chest. "Linden's retired now."

Egor's predatory grin sent a chill down Burner's spine. "You two have history, yes? I think he'll remember you quite well."

Burner's mind reeled as he tried to comprehend what Egor could possibly want with Linden after all these years. And why did Egor believe that Burner could influence Linden in any way?

"My brother will be up for a parole hearing in less than two weeks," Egor said, his voice low and menacing. "You're going to make sure Linden fixes the mess he created. To make sure you do what we say, and you don't try to burn us," he paused, a sarcastic smile playing on his lips, "we'll let your girlfriend live. If not, well, Volk here has been itching to use his knife again."

Egor's cruel smile widened as he took in Burner's reaction. Circling Jenny, he trailed a finger along her tear-stained cheek. "I think we understand each other now, don't we, Mr. Flatts? You'll convince your old friend Linden to help us, or your lovely girlfriend here will pay the price."

Jenny's muffled sobs tore at Burner's heart, her eyes wide with fear. He strained against his bonds, desperate to reach her, to protect her from these monsters. But it was useless. He was trapped, helpless, at the mercy of Egor Novik and his ruthless enforcer.

Volk's rough hands groped and pawed at Jenny as he secured her to the chair, his actions deliberately cruel and provocative. Burner felt a surge of rage and despair, hot tears pricking at the corners of his eyes.

His past sins had finally caught up with him, and now the woman he loved would suffer the consequences of his mistakes.

As Egor and Volk left the room, their cruel laughter echoing in the darkness, Burner slumped in his chair, his head bowed in defeat. He knew what he had to do, knew the price he would have to pay.

He would have to face the one man he'd hoped never to see again, the man who held the key to his salvation and his damnation.

And if he failed, if he couldn't convince Linden to do Egor's bidding, then Jenny would pay the ultimate price. Burner shuddered at the thought, a cold sweat breaking out on his brow.

One thing was certain—his past had finally caught up with him, and there would be no escape this time.

TWO

Chapter 2

THE DESERT LANDSCAPE BLURRED PAST THE CAR WINDOWS. THE SUN hanging low on the horizon penetrated the dust-coated windshield, forcing Hatch to squint. She looked over at Banyan's weary, expressionless face, the endless strip of two-lane highway stretching out before them.

"Not much longer, now." Her offering was met with a grunt.

They'd been driving for the better part of two days since leaving the muggy warmth of Florida's panhandle, exchanging it for the arid but equally hot, if not hotter, Arizona late spring temperatures.

Banyan arched in his seat, his back expelling a loud popping as he did so. "I'm regretting using that rest stop rather than a motel last night. This Jeep is taking its toll on my lumbar."

"You and I have both slept under far worse conditions."

"True. But civilian life's making me soft."

Keep the edge sharp even when it's sheathed. Her dad had said the words more times than she could recount. When she was young, they'd made little sense. In the journey her life had taken, including the path she was on now, the mantra carried more meaning. And with it, her father had once again crossed over into her life. Trails of past wisdom intersecting present circumstances was a hallmark of her existence. Tragedy had stolen him from her. In the years that had passed since his death, she had managed to become closer to her father, holding onto the words of his teachings. The code he'd instilled in her now served as a guidepost. His voice continued to find her ears, and she prayed it always would.

Tedium punctuated the endless stretches of road. The empty vastness of the last hundred miles was interrupted only by the occasional gas station. A sparse network of cacti silhouetted against the brilliant orange of the dipping sun. The air conditioning struggled to keep the scorching heat at bay as the faint scent of hot asphalt and dusty sagebrush seeped through the vents.

A weathered sign appeared on the side of the road, its faded letters revealing the name of their destination: "Welcome to Diamondback - Where the Old West Meets Modern Charm!" On the bottom right corner, the population was listed at 2,187. The numbering was hand painted and, based on the contrast to the wording above, looked as though it had recently been updated. Hatch doubted the change was due to growth. The sign was adorned with a striking rattlesnake coiled around a sparkling diamond, a fitting emblem for the small Arizona town.

"Tracy didn't give me much of an explanation on the reason for the detour. Just said he needed us to do a favor for him." Banyan shrugged. "Said he'd fill us in tomorrow morning."

"In our line of work, favors come with a price."

"Not sure what could be so dire that a town like this would require our services."

"If there's one thing I've come to understand, it's that the size of the town has little to do with the size of the problem." A smattering of images, mostly violent, streamed across her mind. Most of them occurring in small towns, not much bigger than the one they were entering. Not unlike the town where Hatch had grown up.

As the last remaining miles ticked by, Hatch's thoughts drifted to Hawk's Landing and the family she'd left behind. She'd accepted her calling, but it didn't do much to lighten the burden that came with it.

Since making the decision to join Talon Executive Services, Hatch had been conflicted. The private contractor firm who'd once had her in their sights, now had her on their payroll. Had it not been for Jordan Tracy, it was likely Hatch wouldn't have made the leap.

Tracy served as her team leader and he'd proven, on more than one occasion, that he had her back. And with that, he'd earned her trust, a rare commodity in Hatch's world. Ed Banyan was the only other person she'd put on that very short list. There were others, like Cruise and Savage, but they were both gone. Each stolen from her life, under different circumstances, but stolen nonetheless. The void left was a mile-wide chasm and twice as deep.

She hadn't let the thought of Savage enter her mind. Not since their last encounter. The idea of what could've been used to taunt her every step. But it paled in comparison to Cruise's death. The sacrifice he'd made all but consumed her in the wake of that tragic day. She'd fended off the overwhelming grief as long as she could, but after surrendering to it, Hatch was now beginning to find her footing again.

"You in there?" Banyan cocked a smile.

"Huh?" Hatch's surroundings came back into view. "You just got me thinking about home, is all."

"Creature comforts do come calling." A ding sounded from the dash and the low fuel indicator light came on. "Speaking of—nature calls. I'm gonna make a quick pitstop before we find a place to stay."

A couple minutes later, Banyan pulled into a one-pump gas station. Gravel and loose dirt popped under the tires as the vehicle slowed to a stop. The attendant inside looked half asleep.

"I'll pump. You go take care of business." Hatch watched as Banyan put up no resistance and made a beeline for the gas station's restroom.

Hatch took a moment to stretch after stepping out. The phone in her pocket vibrated against her thigh. She half expected it to be Tracy, calling with another update. Hatch was surprised to see it was her mother. The rarity of such an occurrence set her on edge.

"Mom?" Concern furrowed her brow. "Everything okay?"

There was a pause on the other end of the line, followed by a shaky intake of breath. "It's Jed. He's had a heart attack."

"Is he..." Hatch couldn't finish the sentence. For someone who'd experienced so much, seen death in all its forms, saying the word in this circumstance was seemingly impossible. Jed was a Hawk's Landing recluse, living off the grid. A twist of fate brought them together. The gruff old rancher and former paratrooper stood side-by-side with her in a gun battle, saving Hatch's life in the process. Combat forged unbreakable bonds. But the real surprise came when her mother told her that the two were dating. Seeing the love between them and the way he doted on her niece and nephew, taking on the role of father figure to them, made it impossible for Hatch not to accept him into the fold. The thought of losing him was unbearable. And she felt the thin threads of her newfound hold on life coming undone.

"He's in the hospital. Doctors were able to stabilize him."

Hatch released her tension in a long, steady exhale. "Thank God."

"He's not out of the woods yet. They're prepping him for surgery. He's going to need a triple bypass."

Hatch thought of Daphne and Jake, her niece and nephew. The two had lost so much, their young lives marked by tragedy, not unlike Hatch's. Jed had been a welcome return to normal, whatever normal was. "Are the kids okay?"

"Yes. It was actually Jake who found him. And thank goodness he did. Another couple minutes and I might be having a very different conversation with you." Her mother paused as a male voice grumbled something inaudible in the background. "Jed wants to speak to you."

The sound of the muffled exchange of the phone completed, Hatch listened to the labored breathing coming from the other end of the line.

"Hey kid," Jed said between wheezing inhales. "How's things?"

His voice soothed her, relieved her of any worry about more tragedy coming to find her. The gruff, gravelly tone belied the kindness tucked beneath. "I think I'm the one who should be asking you that. How you holding up?"

"They got me hooked up to about every damn thing they could find. I think they're using me to power the microwave."

The chuckle slipping past Hatch's pursed lips helped her relax further. "Sounds like they're taking good care of you."

"Guess so." He huffed. "Looks like the doc wants to climb inside this old rust bucket and wind up my ticker."

"Good. We need you around a little longer."

"They already started in on me about red meat and all that healthy eating. I told them to quit flappin' and flush the engine. Ain't no use in telling me to change my ways. Not like I'm gonna get another seventy years out of this thing." His laugh forced a coughing fit.

Hatch waited quietly for him to settle. "I should be there."

"Why? So you can see me in this dress they got me in?"

"You're family. I should be with you."

"You should be exactly where you are and no place else. This world is meant for the living." He paused to catch his breath. "And you play a very special part in keeping it spinning. Don't worry about me. People like us are built different."

"I think they broke the mold with you." Hatch heard a nurse in the background.

"Gotta go. And don't worry 'bout me. Just another scar to add to my collection."

Hatch felt a tingle run up the twisted branches of the scar extending from her wrist to her shoulder. "I'll be thinking of you."

"I know." Jed cleared his throat. "You keep your head down and watch your six."

"Always do."

With that Jed, was gone.

"Jed's right," her mother said, having taken back the phone. "You do what you have to do. We'll be here when you're done." She heaved a sigh. "I've got to go. You be safe out there. Wherever there is."

"I will. Tell the kids I miss them."

"They know." A pause followed. "I love you, Rachel."

Hatch opened her mouth to speak but her mother had already clicked off.

"Filled her up?" Banyan walked toward the car with two bags of pork rinds cradled in his arm.

"Not yet." Hatch slipped the phone back into her pocket before inserting the pump nozzle into the tank.

His eyes narrowed with concern. "Everything all right?"

"Family emergency. Jed had a heart attack, but he's stable now."

"Sorry to hear. If you need to go home, just say the word. I'm sure that whatever this is, I can go it on my own."

"Not how this works." Hatch's steadiness returned. "Plus, you're not the field operative anymore, remember?"

"Just saying. Tracy would understand. And I don't mind stepping up."

Hatch thought about Cruise. He'd stepped up to save her and the others on that platform. She could picture the last time she laid eyes on him as he slipped into those dark waters. She'd vowed to herself, right then and there, to work alone. Those were the terms of her return to service. Tracy had agreed to them. Banyan was more reluctant and only agreed if she'd let him assist from afar, serving in the role of technical support and overwatch.

"Mission first," Hatch said, taking the pump nozzle out of the fuel filler neck when it clicked.

"You're not in the Army anymore." Banyan gave a half-cocked smile. "But I get it. Old habits die hardest."

"Or not at all."

Banyan nodded, respect flickering in his eyes. "Roger that."

AS THE SKY began to darken and the first stars appeared, they reached the outskirts of Diamondback. The town had a timeless quality, with its dusty streets and weathered buildings that seemed to have been plucked straight from the pages of a Western novel.

The only sign for lodging pointed to a winding road leading away from the center of town. Banyan followed it until pulling into the parking lot of The Jumping Cholla, a run-down motel on the edge of town. The once-vibrant colorful exterior bore the marks of neglect and decay with its peeling paint. A neon sign flickered weakly in the gathering dusk.

They parked in front of the main office and exited the car.

"Looks like this place has seen better days." Banyan popped the trunk and grabbed their bags.

As they made their way to the check-in desk, a dust covered light above the door cast an otherworldly glow on the hacienda-style exterior. The scent of creosote hung heavy in the air, mingling with the faint aroma of diesel from a distant truck stop.

They stepped into the lobby, the tinkling of a bell above the door announcing their arrival. The interior was a kitschy homage to the Old West, with faded murals of cowboy standoffs adorning the walls, their once-vibrant colors now muted by time and the thin layer of dust that clung to every surface. The sand-colored tiles underfoot were scuffed and worn, bearing the marks of countless boots that had traversed the lobby over the years.

A few well-worn leather chairs, their cushions sagging and creased, were arranged in front of a muted TV. On the screen, a pair of newscasters gestured animatedly, their lips moving in silent pantomime, their urgent expressions at odds with the tranquil atmosphere of the lobby. The soft glow of the TV cast long shadows across the room, mingling with the warm light that spilled from the lamps perched on end tables.

On the counter, a coiled rattlesnake sat mounted on a polished wooden base, its scales gleaming under the fluorescent lights. Its glassy eyes stared out into the room, forever frozen in a silent hiss. Hatch's gaze was drawn to the snake's tail, noticing that it was missing its distinctive rattle. The absence of the rattle lent an eerie, unsettling quality to the display, as if the snake was incomplete, its warning silenced.

The air was heavy with the scent of old cigarette smoke and the faint, musty odor of age, a testament to the many years the motel had stood watch over this dusty corner of the desert. Despite the dated decor and the wear and tear of time, there was a certain charm to the lobby, a sense of history and character that seeped from every crack and crevice.

A man exited the backroom and approached the counter. His weathered face was etched with weariness, adding years. "Welcome," he said, his voice crackling like pine on a fire. "Need a place to rest your heads?"

"Two rooms, if you've got 'em." Hatch sauntered up to the desk.

He gave a questioning look, passing between Hatch and Banyan. "Not sure if you could tell from the lot, but we've got plenty of vacancies."

Hatch drew closer and noticed a young girl, no older than ten, nestled in a corner, engrossed in a whispered conversation between two dolls. The child glanced up, her eyes wide and curious, and offered a shy smile before returning to her play. In a flash, she was back home with Daphne, her memory called to the first drawing her niece had made her.

Hatch returned the smile. "Hi," she mouthed.

The motel owner swelled with fatherly pride. "That's my little angel, Camila." The little girl gave a sheepish wave before moving to tuck herself behind him. "She doesn't talk much anymore."

Hatch sensed there was more to the story, a deeper pain lurking beneath the surface of the motel owner's words. She saw it in the tightness of his jaw, the way his eyes flickered with grief. But she didn't press, knowing that some wounds were best left buried.

A faint sound caught her attention. It was a soft, rhythmic rattling, like the gentle shaking of a tiny maraca. Hatch's eyes scanned the room, searching for the source of the noise.

Then she saw it. Clutched tightly in the little girl's hand, partially hidden behind her back, was the missing tail of the rattlesnake. As Camila shifted her weight from foot to foot, the hollow segments clicked together with each movement.

Hatch eyed the mounted snake on the counter, its absent rattle now explained. A faint smile tugged at the corners of her mouth as she imagined the girl carefully detaching the rattle, claiming it as a small trophy or a talisman of bravery.

The motel owner turned and gathered two sets of keys. He slid a dog-eared ledger from under the desk onto the counter between them. "And how will you be paying? We take all forms of credit."

"Do you take cash?" Hatch asked.

"Of course." He smiled. "Mind giving me your names for the record?"

Hatch looked to Banyan. He shrugged.

"No need. Not if you're paying cash." He set the book aside. "How many nights will you be staying?"

"Not sure. Mind if we pay as we go?"

"Fine by me. It's normally sixty a night, but since you're staying in two rooms, I can do forty for each."

"No need for the discount. We'll pay for the rooms we use." Hatch and Banyan set sixty each on the table. She gave a wink to the girl peeking out from behind her father's waist.

They took the keys, each of which was adorned with a cactus-shaped fob. "The name's Ernesto, but people 'round here call me Ernie. You'll find a direct line to the front desk in your rooms. Anything you need, you just hit zero."

They nodded their thanks and headed back out the door. Hatch turned to look behind her at the man and girl behind the front counter, the love shared between them obvious. As well as undeniable sorrow.

Outside, the cool night air was accompanied by a serenade of chirping crickets. They made their way down the sidewalk to their rooms.

"Let's grab some coffee in the morning. I saw that diner down the road." Banyan used the cactus fob to unlock his door.

"Sounds like a plan."

Exhaustion swept over Hatch as she entered her room. The long drive, coupled with Jed's health scare had taken its toll. She plopped down on the old mattress and let herself sink in. Her mind drifted to the unknown of what tomorrow would bring.

Life had prepared her for the unknown challenges. She took solace in knowing that her edge was back, and sharper than ever.

THREE

Chapter 3

THE EARLY MORNING SUN CAST A WARM GLOW OVER THE SPRAWLING
Linden estate, its manicured lawns and pristine façade a testament to
the family's newfound affluence. Inside, Harvey Linden stood at the
kitchen counter, his eyes fixed on the steaming mug of coffee
before him.

Beside him, Max Carver, his right-hand man. He'd come highly
recommended. His military service record was dotted with accommo-
dations and awards, with more than a half dozen deployments under
his belt before taking his skills to the civilian world. Carver told
Linden the decision had been simple. Better pay and fewer people
trying to kill him. Though they came from different worlds, the two
had more in common on that front than Linden cared to let on.

"Something gnawin' at you?" Carver's twenty plus years of military
service didn't diminish his thick Texas twang.

"It's nothing. Just the hearing, I guess."

"No one in their right minds would ever let that savage back out
on the streets. I've peeked at the file."

Linden shot Carver a questioning look.

Carver held his hands up in mock surrender. "Easy boss, part of my job description."

"Your job is to run my security force and serve as my resident expert when consulting with clients."

"True. But none of that pays the bills if my boss is compromised." Carver's tone was a blend of lighthearted banter and honest concern. "If you're worried about something, I'm worried. Just the way it works. And since the governor's office sent you the details on this pardon hearing you've been—for lack of a better word—*tense*."

Linden leaned against the marble countertop, feeling the coolness seep into the moist palms of his hands. He peered out the oversized bay window overlooking the carefully manicured garden, his wife's prized possession since exchanging bustling Phoenix for the isolation the small town of Diamondback offered.

"Six feet of shoveled dirt is the only thing that will keep guys like Anton Novik from stopping their reign of terror."

"Aside from that, I'm sure you'll have no problem convincing the others that man should never see the light of day."

"That's why I was brought in on this one. I'm the one who put him behind bars."

Carver's brow furrowed. "Not exactly sure how things work on the law enforcement side of the house, but doesn't having you on the board call into question the impartialness of your decision?"

"The way it was explained to me is that my personal knowledge of Anton's crimes, both the ones he's been convicted on and the cases he's beat, gives me a vantage point few have." Linden shrugged. "But I do see the counterclaim. Not my call."

"After this is behind you, I'd like to run some thoughts by you on how I can see expanding our security service, transitioning away from the physical and into the digital arena."

"Well, you haven't steered me wrong thus far. But need I remind you, I was better on the street than behind a desk. So you're going to need to do some handholding to get me up to speed on this tech stuff."

"Fair enough."

The sound of footsteps drew their attention to the hallway, where

Linden's wife, Amy, emerged, her designer handbag slung over her shoulder. "I'm heading to the shops. Need anything?"

Linden shook his head, his eyes lingering on the expensive bag. "I felt like you just went shopping. What could we possibly need?"

"I thought you said things are good."

"We are. It's just—"

"Breathe, Harv, we're finally able to splurge a little. After a lifetime of pinching pennies, it feels good to go out and get something I want."

His shoulders slackened. "I guess it'll still take some getting used to."

"I haven't forgotten where we came from. I still remember when we were both working doubles just to keep the lights on." His wife pecked him on the cheek and gave a wink to Carver before spinning on her heels and heading for the door.

He and Angie had spent several years like ships passing in the night. She worked rotating shifts as an ER nurse while he worked the streets, responsible for bringing in many of her patients. It was a gang shooting that had brought them together, a story their kids always got a kick out of. Angie hung up her stethoscope when he took early retirement to pursue his current venture. She traded long hours and blood-soaked scrubs for the easier life. Watching her walk out the door into the bright sunlight, he wondered whether she missed it. God knows he did.

As she breezed out the door, Linden's children, Mia and Ethan, trudged into the kitchen, their backpacks slung over their shoulders. Mia, the elder of the two, heaved a dramatic sigh as she plopped down at the breakfast table.

"I miss my old friends. I hate riding the bus with all these snobby rich kids." She grabbed the carafe of milk and poured it over the bowl of Fruit Loops.

Ethan nodded in agreement. His young face scrunched into a scowl. "Are you driving us this morning?"

"Yes, but we've got to leave a little bit earlier today. I have to drive to Florence this morning."

"Remember when Dad used to drive us to school in the cruiser?" Mia crunched a mouthful of cereal as she spoke. "That was so cool."

"Yeah. Now I have to sit next to Limbo Jimbo on the stupid bus." Ethan pushed at the toast in front of him, making no effort to pick it up.

Linden did his best to pretend the comments, a near constant since making the move, didn't bother him. He thought giving them a bigger house in a better neighborhood would make them happy, that they would appreciate it. This was a lifestyle he'd never thought possible. Coming from a long line of cops, Linden felt he was now living someone else's life, a life he didn't deserve.

"Your dad's got an important job now, too," Carver said. "He may not be driving a police car, but he's still out there keeping people safe. And sometimes, taking on new challenges means making sacrifices." He clapped a hand on the back of Ethan's shoulders. "Better eat up. Your chauffeur will be departing in fifteen minutes."

Linden shot Carver a grateful look, then turned to his children. "I'm not sure what time I'll be finished at the prison today, so Mom will pick you up."

Mia rolled her eyes, a frown formed at the corners of her mouth. "She's always late."

"Cut your mom some slack." Linden had noticed a growing divide between his wife and daughter lately. He was confident it was some sort of preteen angst. Finding his new role as their mediator was akin to his stint as a hostage negotiator for Phoenix PD's SWAT team. There were times he'd rather be talking down a deranged barricaded suspect than a blowout in his own home.

Linden gathered his file on Anton Novik and transferred his coffee into a travel mug. He twirled his finger in the air. "We're rolling out."

Carver pulled the sleek black Range Rover Sentinel to the front door. Linden called this armored version of the luxurious SUV his one personal splurge item. He justified the expense by citing the enhanced protection against various threats. It featured bulletproof glass, reinforced chassis, and run-flat tires. Carver had told him it was a popular choice for high-profile individuals and security professionals.

Linden closed the door and waved to his gardener, Miguel Santiago, who was busy pruning silvery gray leaves of the Texas Sage bushes lining the front exterior of the home. Santiago smiled and tipped his hat with the pruning shears in his hand.

Mia and Ethan climbed into the backseat. Linden ensured they were buckled before entering the passenger's seat. As he closed the door, the phone in the breast pocket of his blazer vibrated. He fished it out, swiped the screen, and opened his messages. The incoming text was from an unknown number.

Tapping it, his pulse quickening as he read the message on the screen.

This isn't a game. Do what you're told. Or there will be consequences.

Carver turned on the ignition and looked over. "The hearing stuff again?"

Linden's jaw tightened. "Just a blast from the past."

"Anything I should be concerned about?"

Linden shook his head. "No. Just someone I hadn't expected to hear from."

"Then I guess we best get a move on." Carver adjusted the rearview mirror and smiled at the kids seated behind him. "Don't want you two yahoos to be late to school."

The Range Rover moved along the quaint neighborhood of their new town. Linden stared out the window, his thoughts drifting from the hearing to the message he'd received. He tried distracting himself with the near constant banter of his children. Nothing could.

Linden couldn't shake the feeling in his gut. The one that had saved his butt many times before was warning him once again.

FOUR

Chapter 4

HATCH LAY ON THE BED, HER BODY SINKING INTO THE MATTRESS AS SHE stared at the ceiling. She had been awake for an hour, but the fatigue from the long drive had kept her from rising. Despite her physical exhaustion, her mind refused to rest, replaying the horrors and tragedies of her past in vivid detail.

She had managed to get a few hours of fitful sleep, but the thin, sheer curtains of the motel room did little to block out the intense rays of the early morning desert sun. The light seeped into the room, casting a harsh glow across the floor and walls.

Army life taught the benefits of being an early riser. There was truth to the old advertising campaign. Soldiers did get more done before 9 AM than most did all day. Although she was no longer a soldier by trade, the routine was ingrained into her, as was running. The health benefits were the bonus. Pounding the pavement every morning was Hatch's form of therapy, a way for her to suppress those memories back into the depths of her mind.

She exited her motel room and was greeted by Ernie repotting a plant in front of the main office.

"Good morning." Ernie waved at her with a soil-stained hand.

"Morning." Hatch saw the same weariness in his eyes from last night. She wondered what kept him up at night, what demons haunted him. Beads of sweat trickled down his forehead. Hatch wondered if he used the morning's toil to clear his mind.

"Going out for a run?"

Hatch worked the kinks out of her legs, lifting her knees, kicking her feet back. "Figured I'd try to beat the heat."

"Too late for that. Got to get up before the sun if you want to keep cool. Not a cloud in the sky. Gonna be a scorcher today." Ernie adjusted the wide brim of his hat and cast his gaze upward. "You might see my daughter on your way out. She likes to play in the fields. If you do, tell her it's time for breakfast."

"I better get moving then."

"Keep to the roads. The rattlers like to warm themselves in the early hours of the day."

"Will do. Thanks for the heads up." Hatch flexed her quads, dipping into a lunge before setting off.

Hatch took to the road. She headed from the motel in a direction that took her away from the town. Running was the best medicine when it came to clearing her head. The news about Jed's condition made for a restless night of sleep. When she'd woken up this morning, her mother had messaged her that he'd made it through the triple bypass surgery and was in recovery. Hatch had breathed a sigh of relief, but the guilt of not being there in her family's time of need had plagued her thoughts. But with each footfall, a little bit of the burden fell from her in the form of the sweat dripping freely.

Ernie hadn't lied. The sun was unforgiving, even in the early morning hours. The only reprieve came by way of the occasional mesquite or cypress trees lining the roadside. The road curved and took her headlong into the rising ball of fire. Disregarding the motel owner's warning, Hatch ditched the road for a dirt path. She traded being blinded by the sun for the potential chance of running into a snake.

High above, a Gila woodpecker's rolling 'churr' call—reminiscent of a dog's squeaky toy—drew Hatch's attention to the towering saguaro cactus where the bird perched. Other than that, the only sound was the bottom of her sneakers padding the dry dirt ground. She focused on controlling her breathing, settling into the rhythmic pace, pushing herself just hard enough to feel the exertion, but not so much that she missed the beauty of the surrounding landscape.

The area surrounding the motel was relatively flat, but it wasn't long before she found herself winding uphill and through red tinged boulders. Hatch used the rock faces as balance points while navigating the uneven terrain.

Several minutes later, she broke through to the crest and slowed to a stop. The sun was at her back. Its punishing rays worked to wick the sweat from her t-shirt. Dust clung to her skin, carried by a light breeze whistling its way along the outcropping of rocks where she stood.

The wind subsided as quickly as it had come. A quiet only possible in remote areas such as this took hold. Hatch embraced the peace of the moment. A quiet mind and ready hand are the weapons of every warrior. She sought to steel her mind to the whirlwind of thoughts circulating within. She closed her eyes and inhaled deeply.

The silence was shattered by a strange cry. Hatch's eyes shot open and scanned the area for the source. In the open expanse surrounding her, it was hard to pinpoint the location. Her first thought was that it was another bird call.

The next time she heard the cry rise from the desert landscape, Hatch knew this was no bird. A shrill "Help!" sent several nearby birds into the air. Hatch saw a curled mass on the ground nearby.

Without a second's hesitation, Hatch bounded down the path in reckless disregard for her own safety. She moved in a dead sprint, dry branches of the shrubs lining her path thrashed her legs. Hatch barely registered the sting as she raced forward.

Once close enough, Hatch was able to make out the form. It was a child, a little girl in a purple flowered sundress. A low whimper accompanied the girl's writhing.

Just as Hatch was about to drop to a knee beside her, she saw the source of the girl's agony. A rattlesnake slithered alongside. The girl scooted, kicking at the snake.

The rattler recoiled. Its tail shook. The diamond-shaped head rose up, its body arcing back in preparation for another strike.

Hatch came in from the side. Her hand launched onto the snake as if fired from a cannon. She felt the cool scales against the web of her left hand as she lifted the reptile off the ground, its body writhing wildly against her grip.

The snake's mouth opened wide, its fangs exposed. Hatch squeezed hard, ratcheting tighter and ensuring the venomous bite didn't find purchase. She stepped away from the child while keeping the snake at bay. Its thick body convulsed, and the tail wrapped itself around Hatch's arm.

Hatch jogged until she was a safe distance away from the child. She scanned her surroundings, searching for a way to release the snake without endangering herself or the girl. Spotting a long, sturdy stick near a small pile of rocks, she carefully reached for it with her free hand, keeping her eyes locked on the snake.

With the stick now in her grasp, Hatch slowly lowered herself to the ground, her movements deliberate and cautious. She eased the snake toward the rocks, its body still writhing against her grip. Hatch used the stick to pin the snake's head to the dirt, just behind its jawline. The snake hissed and thrashed, but the firm pressure of the stick kept its deadly fangs at bay.

Holding the stick steady with one hand, Hatch slowly loosened her grip on the snake's neck with the other. She held her breath as she carefully wriggled her fingers free, one by one. The snake's scales were smooth and cool beneath her touch, its muscles coiling and flexing as it struggled against the restraint.

As soon as her hand was clear, Hatch tightened her hold on the stick, pressing the snake more firmly against the ground. She knew she had to work quickly and carefully to avoid being bitten. With a swift, decisive motion, she lifted the stick and stepped back, allowing the snake to slither into the safety of the rocks. The snake's rattle echoed through the air. Hatch let out a shaky breath.

The girl groaned, weaker than before. Hatch raced back and dropped to her side. Ernie's daughter Camila looked up at her with tear-filled eyes. The little girl's hands clutched at her right leg just below the knee.

"It's going to be alright." Hatch rested a gentle hand on the girl's head. "I'm going to get you to someone who can help. I just want to take a look first, okay?"

Camila nodded. Her chin quivered. Tears left clear streaks along her dirt-covered face.

On the outside of her shin were two small puncture marks, about a half inch apart. The wounds were difficult to see, obscured by swelling and bleeding. The skin surrounding the puncture marks had a reddish coloring that had begun turning to a darker purple color. Hatch was no stranger to snake bites. While not all were venomous, this was not a "dry bite" as was evident by rupture due to the toxic effects.

Hatch pressed on the upper thigh above the knee. "Does this hurt?"

Camila shook her head.

"That's good. That means that the venom hasn't spread that far yet. I don't want you to worry. Staying calm is the most important thing you can do right now." Hatch gave her the same tender look she would've given Daphne. "You're a tough one, huh?"

The little girl gave a weak smile.

"I'm going to need you to be." Hatch bent low, cradling the girl under her neck. She gently slid her right arm under her legs at the knee. "Hold on to my neck. I'm going to have to carry you. It's going to be a bumpy ride."

Camila draped an arm over Hatch's shoulder and weakly gripped the collar of her shirt.

Hatch stood, hoisting the girl as she did. She cradled Camila in her arms and kept her body tight to hers, hoping to alleviate some of the pain caused by the jostling. Hatch then began running again. She put the discomfort of the added weight out of her mind, focusing on her surefootedness.

The return route back to the motel was more direct than her initial trek, but it didn't take away the exertion required to haul a child the near mile and a half over uneven terrain. By the time Hatch was on the paved asphalt, she was drenched in sweat. Camila's grip had grown weaker. Her tanned skin was paler.

Hatch pushed her pace. The motel materialized in the distance. Heavy footfalls announced her approach. The girl's thigh had rubbed against the scar on her arm, causing it to tingle. All of those were mere inconveniences. The only thing that mattered was getting Camila medical attention.

She barely registered the door to Banyan's room open as she passed. Hatch heard him speak, but his words were buried beneath her ragged gulps of the dust-infused air. A moment later, she barged through the motel office's doors. Ernie looked up from the desk with a pleasantness that instantly transformed into one of horror at the sight of his daughter.

"Cholla!" Ernie hurdled the desk. He absorbed his daughter from Hatch into his fold. He looked down at her leg. His voice choked. "I told you. I told—"

"I was able to get to her soon after the bite." Hatch looked at the girl's leg again. "The swelling has spread above the knee. We need to get her to the hospital."

"Too far." Ernie was already making his way to the door just as Banyan entered. "Local doc is closer. He'll have antivenom on hand."

Banyan held the door open. Hatch followed close behind Ernie. She maintained eye contact with Camila. The girl's breathing became more labored. She made a weak attempt at a smile as her father laid her across the backseat of his older model Honda.

Ernie shut the door and jumped into the driver's seat. "Thank you."

Hatch nodded. The tires kicked up a plume of dirt as the car sped away toward town. A quiver of exertion spread from her legs to the rest of her body.

Banyan stood alongside her. He took stock of her current state and shook his head. "I've been around the world. Seen some crazy shit. But I don't think I've ever met a lightning rod for chaos like you."

"Maybe someone upstairs is testing me?" Hatch made a half-hearted attempt to swipe the dirt and debris from her clothing.

"Well, if that's the case, I'd say you're acing them." Banyan smiled. "You in the mood for food?"

"You have no idea." Hatch looked down at Camila's blood dotting her shirt. "Give me a minute to get cleaned up."

She stepped inside the motel room, the door closing behind her with a soft click. The room was small and dimly lit, with a faint musty odor that clung to the air. The worn carpet beneath her feet had seen better days, its once-vibrant pattern now faded and stained. Against the far wall, an ancient air conditioner sputtered to life, its battle rattle echoing through the room as it began its day-long war against the oppressive desert heat. The unit shuddered and groaned, struggling to pump cool air into the stuffy space.

Hatch made her way to the bathroom, her footsteps muffled by the thin carpet. She turned on the shower, letting the water run until it reached a comfortable temperature. As she stepped under the stream, the cool water cascaded down her back, washing away the grime and sweat of the day's earlier events. The steady patter of the droplets against the tiled floor created a soothing rhythm, a momentary respite from the early morning's chaos.

As she lathered her hair with the motel's generic shampoo, Hatch's mind wandered, pondering the purpose behind their presence here in this sleepy desert town. With so much still unknown, she couldn't help but wonder what other tests and challenges lay in wait, lurking just beneath the surface of this seemingly peaceful place.

FIVE

Chapter 5

LINDEN LOOKED AT HIS WATCH FOR THE SECOND TIME IN FIVE MINUTES, as if constant checking would expedite their arrival. After dropping the children off, they'd managed to get waylaid by a traffic jam exacerbated by the morning commuters heading into Phoenix. The delay added thirty minutes to the typical ninety-minute commute. With each passing second, Linden felt his blood pressure increase in kind.

"Almost there." Carver adjusted the visor to deflect the sun's glare.

"I hate being late." Traffic was a mess, the sea of brake lights adding to the stress of the ominous warning he'd received earlier.

"Technically, you're not. You've still got fifteen minutes."

"I've still got to go through the rigmarole at the security desk."

"I thought all you ex-cops had some type of secret handshake to cut the lines."

"Maybe if this was Phoenix." Linden fiddled with the case file in his hand. "But this is Florence, and my credentials amount to jack squat."

"Don't sweat it too much. You're in charge. The clock doesn't start until you say so."

Linden silently rehearsed the procedural aspect of his role as the presiding official as Carver turned left onto East Butte Avenue. Ahead on the right-hand side was the Arizona State Prison Complex. The imposing facility sprawled outward, an oasis for the state's worst offenders, set against the desert landscape. Tall chain-link fences topped with coiled razor wire surrounded the perimeter. The fence line was punctuated by watchtowers manned by armed guards, providing constant surveillance of the grounds below.

The prison complex itself consisted of several buildings of varying sizes, mostly constructed from dull, gray concrete blocks. The muted tones blended with the sand-swept surroundings. Sparse windows gave it its distinct institutional appearance.

The main entrance to the prison was heavily fortified, with a secure gate system and additional fencing. Visitors and staff were required to pass through this checkpoint. Correctional officers manned the station, monitoring all comings and goings.

Carver followed the signs, guiding them to a paved parking lot near the entrance designated for visitors. Carver parked in a spot facing the main building. Linden barely allowed the vehicle to come to a complete stop before he opened the door to exit.

"Give 'em hell, boss. I'll be here when you're finished."

Linden shut the door and gave a two-fingered salute before hustling off toward the complex's entrance.

He bounded up the concrete steps, taking two at a time. The short jaunt from the car to the main doors left him coated in a thin layer of sweat. The blast of air conditioning was a welcome reprieve as he made his way over to the security station. He was grateful to see only one person ahead of him in line, and they had already stepped through the metal detector.

He checked his watch. It appeared he'd be on time, but barely. It was times like this that he missed wearing the badge. Linden's identification card was clipped to the outside pocket of his suitcoat.

"Good morning, sir. Please place all items in the tray and step through."

Linden took off his watch and placed it into the plastic tray. The back of the watch was etched with his dates of service, a gift from the police union given to him upon his retirement from the force. He set his keys alongside it and slid the tray over to the corrections officer.

The guard was professional, but more importantly, he was efficient. Linden stepped through the rectangular arches of the metal detector and gathered his belongings as they exited the other end of the x-ray machine. "I'm running late to a pardoning hearing. Can you point me in the right direction?"

"Can I have the prisoner's name?"

"Anton Novik."

The guard keyed the lapel mic and relayed the information over the radio. A moment later, a female voice responded with the room number. The guard acknowledged. "It's just down the hall, fifth door on the left."

Linden thanked the corrections officer and hurried off in that direction.

He took a moment to compose himself before opening the windowless door marked Conference Room 8. The last time he faced off with Novik was during the trial. There was no love-lost between them. If the world were truly black and white, this little reunion would only serve to widen that divide.

He clutched the file folder in his arm and wiped the opposite sweaty hand against his pants leg to dry it. Then he opened the door, greeted by the impatient expressions of everyone else who'd made it earlier.

The room was small, measuring about twenty square feet. It had the sterile feel of a doctor's office with stark white walls and a polished gray concrete floor. Fluorescent lights buzzed overhead, casting a harsh, artificial glow throughout.

In the center was a large rectangular table made of heavy, durable wood. Adjustable microphones protruded from the tabletop at each station, designed to record the sessions in progress. Surrounding it were several chairs upholstered in a well-worn, navy-blue fabric.

At one end of the table, a slightly more elaborate chair, was reserved for the presiding official. Linden's name was written in black

Sharpie on a paper trifold. The other board members were already seated. He felt their eyes upon him as he took his seat and faced them.

"Apologies for my late arrival." Linden leaned forward and filled a paper cup with water from a carafe.

"I'm just glad we didn't have to reschedule. Took me a lot of juggling to fit this in." The woman's name tag identified her as Diane Whitmore.

The other members of the hand-picked board remained quiet. Linden made eye contact with each before giving a general nod to the group. "Has everyone had a chance to review the case file regarding the inmate in question?"

A murmured acknowledgment rippled around the table.

A man named Marcus Trevelyan cleared his throat. "I—we—had a question." He looked around the room for approval, which came in subtle nods from the other members. "I guess I speak for the group on this one."

"Go ahead," Linden said.

"We saw that you were the investigating officer in the case against Mr. Novik."

"Yes, I was."

"Isn't it a conflict of interest to have you preside over this hearing?"

"There's nothing in the law that prohibits my involvement." Linden saw Trevelyan open his mouth to speak and cut him off. "But I do understand your concern. I did not volunteer for this position. I was requested by a member of the governor's office to act as the presiding officer in this hearing because of my unique under-standing of the case details and my extensive history with the Novik family."

Trevelyan sat back in his seat. "Thank you for explaining."

"If there are any other questions regarding my status or the case itself, I'd suggest we get them out of the way now." Linden scanned the group. "Okay, let's get on with it, shall we?"

Linden looked over toward the rear of the room. A muscular corrections officer stood beside a solid metal door with a small, rein-forced glass window. From his current vantage point, Linden couldn't see Novik, but he could feel the hate reverberating from inside the cell.

"I'll be going on the record now." Linden pressed the red button to activate the audio recording device in the room. He waited a few seconds to ensure the system had fully activated. He noted the date and time of the hearing as well as recognizing each of the board members present.

"Good morning, everyone. I'm Harvey Linden, Chairperson, and will be presiding over the pardoning hearing for Anton Novik. At this time, we will ask for Mr. Novik to be brought forward so his case may be heard."

Taking his cue, the guard slid his ID card over the access panel. A loud buzz sounded, and the clang of the lock's internal release echoed in the chamber. The guard entered the confines of the small holding cell. A moment later, Anton Novik stepped forward. A long chain extended from his shackled wrists to those at his ankles. The four-point restraints forced him to shuffle. The bright orange, designed to make inmates more visible, only served to add to the Belarusian mob kingpin's menace.

Linden heard someone at the table swallow hard. He didn't shift his attention to look at the source. Instead, he held the gaze of the prisoner who was staring at him with a murderous rage.

The guard seated Novik away from the board members. Close enough to be heard, but far enough away to prevent any chance of physical contact. The guard stood close by him, maintaining proximity control.

The room was cast in an uncomfortable silence. Linden cleared his throat and decided to break it. "Please state your name and inmate number for the record."

Novik responded in a thick accent. "My name is Anton Novik, inmate number 031524."

"We are gathered here today to consider your application for parole that was filed on your behalf. Do you understand the purpose of this hearing?"

"Yes, I do."

"Each member of this board has had an opportunity to review all records related to the crime for which you are currently serving a fifteen-year sentence. Drug distribution and the illegal sale of firearms."

"You sure they have access to all of the records?" Novik ignored the other members of the review board, never taking his eyes off Linden.

"I will reiterate for the record that each member here today has been granted full access to the entirety of records pertaining to the crimes with which you have been charged." Linden turned his attention to the panel. "Is there anyone in this room who feels they were not given a true and complete record? Please state your name and answer for the record."

Each member stated they were satisfied with the case materials provided. Linden breathed a silent sigh of relief. He hesitated in returning his attention to their guest.

Linden cleared his throat and gulped down the cup of water. "The reason you're being considered for early release is due to your cooperation with an ongoing criminal investigation. Is this correct?"

Novik's face drew up into a twisted smile, exposing his smoke-stained teeth. "I'm not at liberty to discuss the specifics of my *cooperation*, but I will say that I have done my civic duty."

Linden knew the truth behind this sudden shift in leniency. He'd heard from an old friend who'd been working on a serial case. The murderer had been arrested, but many of the victim's bodies were not located. The killer, a man by the name of Jankowitz, derived pleasure from the pain this caused the grieving families.

The detective working the case told Linden that Novik had gathered information about the whereabouts of some of the bodies, most of them missing teenage girls. Jankowitz didn't appear to have volunteered this information willingly. The guards found him clinging to life in the prison shower. Shortly thereafter, Novik bartered the deal to share what he knew about the missing girls only if he would be considered for an early parole hearing. Linden had known then, as he did now, there was no altruism involved. Novik's only motive was escaping confinement.

Novik was smart enough to know the leverage this would provide.

Closure for grieving families wins big points. Compared to his drug and gun charges, parole was an easy offering. Linden had peered into the dark abyss that was the soulless man seated before him. He was aware of the viscousness with which the crime lord maintained his throne. Proving it was next to impossible. He vowed to do everything in his power to ensure Anton Novik never saw the light of day.

"At this time, the board would like to extend Mr. Novik an opportunity to make a statement on his own behalf, expressing remorse for his actions and explaining why he believes he deserves a pardon."

"I take full responsibility for my actions, and I am deeply sorry for harm I cause. I come from country torn by war. I come to United States for search of American dream. But instead, I find myself barely surviving. Work, for someone like me, with no education and trouble with language, very hard to find. I do what I can to put food on table and take care of family." Novik broke eye contact and looked down at his feet.

When he looked back up, his eyes were moist. "I know selling drugs wrong. I learn from mistake. During time in prison, I work hard. My English better now. No more crime for me. I going to live a life that follows law. Make world a better place, yes?"

Linden choked back his disgust. He'd been on many a wire when he was working to bring down Novik and knew his English was nearly fluent. He was playing it up in front of his new audience.

He took his eyes off Novik and turned his attention to the room. "Does anyone on the board have any specific questions for this inmate?"

Trevelyan, the de facto spokesperson for the other members, sat forward with genuine interest. "If you are granted a pardon, what are your immediate plans upon release?"

"My brother gets me job at machine shop. This good job. Honorable work. I promise." Novik looked from Trevelyan to Linden. "I keep promises, yes?"

Linden felt the muscles ripple along his clenched jawline. "If there is nothing further from the inmate, all statements have been made and questions answered, the board will deliberate and make a decision on whether to grant the parole." Silence followed. "Very well. The board will now take a brief recess to deliberate. We will reconvene in fifteen minutes to announce our decision."

The guard escorted Novik back to the holding area. The metallic hiss of the lock was music to Linden's ears. The man sealed behind that door should never be allowed back into civilized society. Now his job was to ensure the others seated before him saw it the same way.

SIX

Chapter 6

THE COPPER CACTUS CAFÉ WAS A CHARMING, LOCALLY OWNED DINER just a short walk from Hatch's motel. The exterior was adorned with a large hand-painted sign featuring a stylized cactus wearing a cowboy hat, its vibrant colors standing in contrast to the dry desert backdrop.

Hatch entered through the glass door which displayed the days and times they were open. Hatch allowed herself a moment to embrace the cooler air of the restaurant's interior while her mind, engrained to do so over years of training, scanned the environment for threats.

Banyan followed close behind. "The smell alone is enough to satisfy my hunger."

The interior was a blend of Southwestern decor and classic Americana. The walls were adorned with vintage photographs depicting the area's mining history, as well as colorful portrayals of desert landscapes. Rustic wooden tables and booths accented with turquoise upholstery lined the dining area, while a gleaming chrome countertop and red leather stools added a touch of nostalgia.

The aroma of freshly brewed coffee and sizzling bacon filled the air, mingling with the scent of green chilies and spices. Aside from the clink of silverware and the clatter of porcelain, friendly chatter of locals added to the lively and welcoming atmosphere of the place. Hatch had learned a lot about many different towns just from their eateries. If this held true, then Diamondback was a throwback to a simpler, quieter time.

Hatch settled into a booth, her body sinking into the worn leather of the seat. Banyan tried to contain a yawn as he sat across from her. He immediately turned his mug upright and surveyed his surroundings for the nearest waitress.

A moment later, a woman in her mid-fifties sauntered up with a coffee pot in hand. "Looks like you could use a little of the good stuff?" She gave Banyan a playful wink.

"You read my mind." Banyan extended his cup as if he was Oliver begging for more porridge.

"I'll second that." Hatch slid her cup over to the end of the table and watched as the woman filled it.

The waitress, whose nametag read Sue, set out two oversized laminated menus on the table between them. She set the coffee pot down and pulled out an order pad from her turquoise apron.

Hatch took a second to run her eyes over the menu. Everything looked delicious. Between the run and the adrenaline dump experienced when rescuing Ernesto's daughter, Hatch had worked up a lumberjack's appetite.

"This your first time at The Triple C?" Sue chewed a piece of gum as she spoke.

"Yes," Hatch replied. "Just passing through."

"Well, you came to the right place. When it comes to breakfast, nobody does it better." She looked over her pad at them. "It's all good. But if you want to get a true taste of the local flavor, I'd recommend the Sonoran Sunrise Omelet. It's a house specialty, and my personal favorite."

Hatch read felt her stomach rumble as she read the description: *A hearty omelet filled with chorizo, diced potatoes, fire-roasted green chilies, and melted cheddar cheese. Topped with a zesty red salsa and served with warm corn tortillas.*

"Sold." She set the menu aside.

"Don't think you'll be disappointed." Sue grabbed Hatch's menu and turned her attention to Banyan, leaning in a little closer. "If you're in the mood for something a little sweeter, I'd go with the Prickly Pear Pancakes. My daughter grew up on 'em. You get three pancakes in a stack of the fluffiest buttermilk pancakes you've ever had. We infuse each with the sweet, tart flavor of prickly pear cactus fruit. It's served with a side of prickly pear syrup and a dollop of whipped butter."

"You must be a mind reader." Banyan returned the waitress' smile. He gulped down his coffee and helped himself to another cup before she scurried off.

"Well, whatever Tracy's got in store for us, at least we'll face it on a full stomach." Hatch added a spoonful of sugar to her coffee. She normally liked it black, but after the exertion, she needed to replace her glycogen stores. "Have you heard anything about what this is all about?"

"Not yet. He should be calling in a bit. I sent him a text while you were out on your run." Banyan fished into his backpack and pulled out his laptop. "Figured while we wait, I could show you something I've been working on."

"Is this your latest and greatest doohickey?"

"I don't know about greatest. Still working out some kinks." He powered up the laptop and then punched in an access code before turning it so Hatch could see.

Hatch saw his cursor hover over an icon. It looked like the letter O surrounded by a bunch of lightning bolts. "What am I looking at?" she asked.

"It's not about looking." Banyan plugged in a headset and handed it to Hatch. "It's about listening."

Hatch slipped the headset on. The soft pads enclosed her ears and the noise of the diner disappeared. She watched as Banyan double-clicked the icon.

The silence of the preceding seconds was replaced by voices, each clear as though they cupped their hands over her ear and were speaking directly to her. And then more voices joined in until it was an overwhelming cacophony of barely interpretable words, as if someone had taken an audible recording of the dictionary and tossed it into a blender.

Hatch's heart raced as the barrage of voices assaulted her senses. Her mind reeled, struggling to process the onslaught of information. A wave of panic washed over her, and she felt her breath catch in her throat. The voices seemed to grow louder with each passing second, threatening to drown out her own thoughts.

Desperate for relief, she reached for the headset to remove it, her hands fumbling with the device. She needed to escape the chaos, to find a moment of peace amidst the auditory storm.

Banyan smiled and held up a finger. Hatch obliged as he punched something into the keyboard, feeling a headache oncoming.

Hatch endured the assault on her eardrums and noticed one by one, the voices dropped off until there was only one. It was a female's, one Hatch recognized as Sue, their waitress. She spun her head and saw the woman standing off to the side of the kitchen area. She had her phone up to her ear and Hatch could hear her, clear as day. "...You told me you'd cut me a break. Just keep the power running until I get off shift. I told you I don't have the extra fifty, but I'll see if I can get it by the end of the day. Pl—" Her voice stopped mid-sentence. Hatch turned back to Banyan and saw he'd closed the app.

She slid the headphones off and took a sip of her coffee, allowing her mind to settle and her ears to adjust. Sue was off the phone now. Hatch watched the woman as she took a moment to compose herself before stepping back into sight of the customers.

"What do you think?" Banyan asked.

"I think you just violated everyone's sense of privacy." Hatch smirked and rubbed at her ears as though she were trying to scrub away the lingering conversations. "What was that?"

"I call it the Omnisphere. In a nutshell, it's a cutting-edge mobile application that revolutionizes surveillance and intelligence gathering." Banyan leaned forward and lowered his voice. "The app uses the user's smartphone as a central hub to create a localized mobile wire network that can intercept and monitor cellular communications within a specific radius. For this demonstration, I used my laptop, but I've already created a version for cellphone use."

He continued, "Omnisphere sends out a specialized signal that mimics a cell tower, tricking nearby phones into connecting to it. Once connected, the app can intercept and decrypt the data transmitted by these devices, including voice calls, text messages, and even internet traffic."

"Isn't there a bunch of legal red tape for something like this? I can only imagine the long line of lawyers who'll be ready to fight this one."

"Maybe. Maybe not." Banyan shrugged. "Depends."

"On what?"

"Who's using it?"

Hatch finished the last of her coffee. "Hopefully, it remains in the hands of the good guys."

"There are variations of similar products out there. What sets Omnisphere apart is its ability to operate undetected, leaving no trace on the targeted devices. The app employs advanced encryption and stealth protocols to ensure its activities remain invisible." Banyan closed his laptop and slid it back inside his backpack. "Still working on some of the bugs, but it's almost there."

"Ever think of taking this little side hustle stuff of yours to market?" Hatch asked. "You could probably make some decent cash. Then there's the added bonus of less likelihood of getting killed."

"What's the fun in that?"

"You've got a pretty twisted idea of fun."

"Says the girl who can't go for a morning jog without tripping over a shitstorm."

Sue returned with a large tray perched on her shoulder and a full pot of coffee in her other hand. "Sorry 'bout the wait."

"No problem." Hatch was greeted by the savory combination wafting up from the plate of food set in front of her. "Looks incredible."

"Could I trouble you for some more of that coffee?" Banyan asked, after gulping down a mouthful of the pancakes. "Your daughter was right. These are amazing!"

Sue smiled as she filled their cups. Hatch noticed that she struggled to hide the distress and wondered if she would've noted the change in demeanor had she not eavesdropped on the waitress.

"Let me know if you need anything else. I'll be around. Just holler." She turned and began making her rounds.

Hatch dug into her omelet. She had devoured half of it before Banyan's cellphone began vibrating on the tabletop. She could see the incoming call was from Jordan Tracy.

SEVEN

Chapter 7

Linden worked his eyes around the table. He applied his adept skill at reading the non-verbal communication of body language, a skill honed over the years of interviews he'd conducted as a detective. You could tell a lot in the things not said, often more accurately than the things that were. Whitford broke eye contact almost as soon as he'd made it. That was a problem. She couldn't meet his gaze, meant she was conflicted, likely about the veiled insinuations Novik made during his testimony. She was now pretending to review the file in front of her.

He made a mental note to ease her worry. Part of being an expert interrogator was to build rapport with the other side, make them feel a sense of kinship. This enabled the facilitation of communication and, in some circumstances, its manipulation. He needed her on his side.

Trevelyan made no attempt to hide his disdain for Linden. He could tell his initial misgivings at having the lead detective serve as head of this parole hearing were further exacerbated after hearing Novik's side of things. With a guy like Trevelyan, there was no point in playing patty cakes. He was a gruff, unhappy man. Linden knew the direct approach was likely to yield the best possible results.

"Say what you're thinking. This is not the time or place to hold your tongue." Linden leveled his comment at Trevelyan. He noticed Whitford shift in her seat.

"Seems like there's a history between you and Mr. Novik, that I am certain of." Trevelyan rolled his sleeves up, exposing the thick layer of dark hair covering his forearms, which he folded against his chest. "What that means exactly... seems suspect."

"You're taking his word for it?" Linden's temper flared, his frustration spreading across his flushed cheeks. "Do you have any idea how many inmates claim they're innocent? A judge and jury convicted him."

"Based on a case you investigated."

Linden's eyes narrowed. "If you've got an accusation, make it."

"Did you tamper with any aspect of this case?" Trevelyan tapped his finger on the file folder to his right.

"No. I did not." Linden let out a long slow breath. "I understand it is our job to look at this potential release as objectively as possible, but—"

"Exactly my point. There's no way you can be objective."

Linden held up a hand. "Let me finish. Objectivity is the goal, but I'm here to ensure that nothing masks the true nature of the man seated in the cell over there."

"He sounded as though he's given some thought to his mistakes." Whitford's voice squeaked.

"A speech he's rehearsed a thousand times prior to this day." Linden softened his tone in speaking with her. "Bet you couldn't tell from his performance, but Anton Novik is capable of speaking perfect English. Truth be told, he's fluent in several dialects."

Whitford opened her mouth and then closed it again without uttering a word, only offering a discontented sigh.

"And that is why I've been selected to preside over this hearing. Don't feel bad. He's a master manipulator. How do you think he evaded law enforcement as long as he did?" Linden noticed this lightened her mood.

"Which brings us back to the case you were able to put on him." Trevelyan poured a cup of coffee from a nearby carafe. He blew at the steam before taking a sip, all the while never taking his eyes off Linden.

Linden stared the man down as he spoke. "Do you know how long I worked to bring him down? Years of my life spent trying to piece together enough evidence to prove to a jury what I had learned through countless investigations and numerous eyewitness accounts."

"And what happened to those cases?"

"I'm not the one up for parole. But if you really want to know, most of those cases never saw the light of day."

"And why's that?"

"Because those witnesses were either too scared to testify or...or they disappeared."

"Are you saying that Mr. Novik killed those people?" Whitford seemed shocked at the accusation.

"You don't get to the top of a criminal syndicate by being a nice guy. The steps to the top are lined with the bodies of those who stand in their way."

"Of all those investigations, all those alleged murders, the only one that stuck was a drug and gun case?" Trevelyan was less hostile now. His tone was more of genuine interest.

"Capone was brought down for tax evasion," Linden said. "His legacy of violence never felt the hand of justice."

Trevelyan fixed Linden with a puzzled look. "Are you seriously comparing Anton Novik to Al Capone?"

"If we're making comparisons, I'd say Novik is in a league of his own." Linden paused, noting that both Whitford and Trevelyan hung on his every word. It had taken some effort, but he had their undivided attention. Now it was time to drive the point home. "He makes witnesses disappear. One of them was a fifteen-year-old girl named Alyssa Park. I could never prove it, but I have no doubt he was responsible. When we finally found her, there were only pieces left."

The silent exchange between Trevelyan and Whitford told Linden everything he needed to know. Their decision was made. The denial was at hand. He thought about the message he'd received earlier that day. And the one he'd received when first notified about the hearing. Neither would stop him from doing the right thing. He closed his eyes for a moment, the image of Alyssa's mangled body flashed across his mind. He had vowed then he would do what it took to bring Anton Novik to justice. Linden would honor that promise once more.

"You make a compelling case," Trevelyan said.

Whitford tapped the manila folder in front of her. "You seem to know far more about this inmate than either of us could glean from this file. I trust your judgment. If you say he stays, you have my support."

"This decision needs to be unanimous, or it'll get shuffled off to appeals." Linden directed his statement at Trevelyan.

Trevelyan shrugged. "Doesn't sound like this guy's going to get out and start running charities. He stays."

Linden swiveled in his chair toward the guard standing by the cell door. "We're ready to inform the prisoner of the board's decision."

The guard slid open the heavy cell door. The familiar rattle of chains echoed through the small room's interior as Novik made his way across the floor and took his seat. The career criminal maintained the façade of the wrong man made right, a victim of the system looking for a second lease on life. He settled his gaze on the man seated at the head of the table.

Linden reached over and activated the recording device. "After final review of the case facts leading to the incarceration for which parole has been requested, and the careful consideration of the testimony presented today, the board has decided to deny Anton Novik, Inmate Number 031524, a pardon. This decision is based on findings of this panel and were not made under any duress or coercion."

A low rumble resonated from Novik. His eyes no longer feigned hope, replaced by pure, unadulterated rage. The contempt was directed at one man. "You think this is the end? You think you've won?"

"Please remove Mr. Novik from the presence of this board." Linden's delivery was calm and professional, an intentional contradiction to the behavior exhibited by his sworn enemy.

The guard lifted Novik from his seat. The shackles clanged as the inmate twisted from the guard's hold. For a brief moment, it looked as though he was going to make a beeline for Linden. Instead, he pointed his finger in his direction. His broken English seemed to have fixed itself. "This will cost you in ways you've never dreamed of."

Linden inwardly relished in the outburst of the man he'd kept in prison. "For the record, let it be shown that Mr. Novik is making a direct threat toward the parole board."

"Not the board." Novik's eyes darkened and a wicked smile formed. "Just you."

The guard snatched Novik, gripping him on the shoulder and leather belt of the restraining harness. He shoved Novik forward toward the open cell.

The steel closed and the orange jumpsuit disappeared into the holding area beyond. A heavy silence fell over the three members seated around the table.

"Any final words before I end the recording?" Linden asked. Seeing the solemn shake of their heads, he switched off the device.

Trevelyan offered an apologetic look. "Sorry I ever questioned you. That guy's definitely a monster."

"Like I said, he's a great actor. But make no mistake, you've just seen the wolf beneath the sheep's clothing."

"Thank you." Whitford's voice was no louder than a whisper.

"For what?"

"For getting a man like that off the streets."

"It's one of the few arrests I've made that truly gives me peace." Linden lied. He'd lost more sleepless nights to Anton Novik than he'd ever admit to. It was one of the reasons he'd taken early retirement, hoping to put some distance between that world and his.

"He's going to appeal again. You know that, right?" Trevelyan pushed back his chair and stood.

"And I'll be here every time, making sure he serves the full term of his sentence."

The board members exchanged pleasantries and said their good-byes. Trevelyan made a point of trying to clear the air between them before departing. Linden hung back for a few minutes. He wanted to put some lag time between him and the other two, not wanting to continue their conversations beyond the walls of this conference room.

Linden collected his case file and tidied up the room, pushing in the chairs beneath the table before making his way to the door. He looked back at the cell. The large guard stood in front of the small window, blocking any view of its interior. He exited into the hallway, hoping this would be the last time he ever saw Anton Novik.

He made his way down the hall to the security station at the front door. The guard who'd pointed the way gave a nod. "Looks like he'll be a guest in your fine establishment a bit longer," Linden said.

The guard laughed. "Better our house than yours."

Linden smiled and exited the building. He'd lived in Arizona his whole life but exchanging air conditioning for the dramatic temperature shift of the outdoors never ceased to shock his system. He took a moment to adjust, already feeling sweat start to form along his spine. His pocket vibrated. He looked down at the message.

You should've listened.

EIGHT

Chapter 8

THE AROMA OF THE DINER HAD GROWN SWEETER THANKS TO THE prickly pear syrup of Banyan's meal. Hatch could almost taste it in the coffee she drank. She edged herself toward the center of the table near the phone set between them.

Banyan reached into his bag, pulled out a small black case, and unzipped it. He handed Hatch one of the earbuds. "Standby. Gonna take you off speaker."

"Hope you two are enjoying Arizona," Tracy said, his voice coming through loud and clear in Hatch's right ear. "I appreciate you helping me out with this one."

"Least I could do." Hatch continued to eat as she spoke, too hungry for manners to slow her down. "You've always had my back. It's nice to be able to return the favor."

Banyan slathered a forkful of pancake with the dark syrup before stuffing it in his mouth, also apparently undeterred by manners. "You said this was a low-key op?"

"Max Carver, an old Army buddy of mine, reached out. He's a

senior member of a small private security firm in the area. He became concerned his employer might be targeted by some heavy hitters."

The heat from the fire-roasted green chillis tickled the back of her throat. "His employer on the up and up?"

"From what Carver tells me. He's a retired cop. Name's Harvey Linden. I did some cursory digging. He's decorated. Had some major busts, one of which got a lot of press. Took down a big-time mob boss."

"And you think it's related?"

"Don't know. Carver will fill you in. He's taking his boss to a parole hearing in Florence now and will call you when he's free."

"Doesn't sound like Carver told his boss he was looking into this." Hatch tore a piece of warm tortilla and scooped up some of the fresh salsa.

"Correct. Linden isn't aware." Tracy cleared his throat. "Carver's a professional. He's a 'measure twice, cut once' kind of guy."

"Sounds like we're going to be his measuring tape," Banyan said between bites.

"If it's nothing, you get a couple days of rest and relaxation in small town Arizona."

"And if it's not?" Hatch asked.

"Then you forward whatever you find over to Carver and he'll handle it through official channels. This is an intel-gathering operation only. No need to kick the hornets' nest on this one."

"Good to hear." Hatch could still feel the lingering aches and pains from her brutal encounter in Panama City. Her body, battered and bruised from the relentless hand-to-hand combat in the confines of a helicopter, was slowly on the mend. A few days of light intel work sounded like the perfect prescription for her recovery.

"Did you get a chance to show her the program you've been working on?" Tracy asked.

"Just did."

"What'd you think, Hatch?"

"It's impressive, that's for sure. Ethical? Jury's still out."

"This might be a good opportunity to field test it," Tracy said.

Banyan leaned back and grinned ear to ear. "You just read my mind."

"I'm sure that'll be the next app you build." Hatch smirked back.

"I'm going to patch Carver in and then I've got to run. Let me know if you need anything on my end. Again, I appreciate it."

There was a click, the line went silent, and a few seconds later Tracy's voice was replaced by another. "I'm partial to face-to-face introductions. Apologies. I'm a bit of a chauffeur this mornin'."

Hatch noted a thick accent, maybe Texas. "No problem. Happy to help. Tracy speaks highly of you."

"Don't know about all that, but he sure does sing your praises. Sounds like we've all played in the same sandbox, albeit at different times." He cleared his throat. "I knew your father."

Hatch felt that familiar unease, the kind that often-accompanied encounters with her father's former associates. The memory of Talon's betrayal, of their attempt to silence her father and then her, still lingered in the back of her mind. Though she now worked for the very organization she once despised, the past had a way of casting long shadows. "Were you in his unit?"

"Wish I had been. But no. We did cross paths a time or two. Hell of a soldier. That compliment comes from men who aren't prone to giving 'em."

Hatch poked at her plate with her fork. "I'll take it as high praise then."

"From what Tracy told us, your boss might be in some kind of trouble. Is that right?" Banyan asked.

"Looks that way. Exactly what and how bad are still a bit unclear."

"Why don't you tell us what you know, and we can try to figure out how best to help." Hatch was grateful the conversation had shifted from personal back to professional, a much more comfortable territory for her.

"Not sure exactly how much Tracy filled you in on. But my boss Harvey Linden is a retired detective out of Phoenix. He's got an impeccable record. Took a bullet while stopping an armed robbery some years back. Could've taken the medical retirement but stayed on."

"Why?" Hatch had taken the medical. An option which she'd fought tooth and nail to avoid, only accepting it after the team she'd served on rejected her attempts at returning to full duty. It was a decision that continued to haunt her.

"He told me he had unfinished business. He'd gone toe-to-toe with some mob guys. The way he tells it, bringing them down became his obsession."

"Sounds like it was personal," Banyan said.

"What isn't? Hell, how many firefights got personal for people like us? Just the way of things."

"Is this the guy he took down? Tracy mentioned a heavy hitter," Hatch said.

"Anton Novik's the guy's name. From what Linden's told me, which isn't much, this guy was a real piece of work. You name a crime, and it sounds like he's committed it."

"Linden put him behind bars, and you think they're looking to even the score?"

"If I knew that answer, I wouldn't have called. A few weeks ago, Linden got assigned to run a parole review board. Bet you can guess who it was for."

"Novik?" Banyan asked.

"You got it."

"That seems like it would be against some guidelines or something," Hatch said. She'd served on similar boards while in the Military Police, but never regarding one of her own cases.

"I said the same thing. He said it's not commonly done, but there are no rules against it."

"Did he say how he got picked? Or why?"

"No. He'll talk cop shop on just about any case except for the Novik stuff. He's pretty tight-lipped about it."

"Do you think he asked to be on it?" Hatch asked.

"Possibly. Maybe he wanted to make sure this turd stayed flushed."

"Seems reasonable enough to me." Banyan wiped some of the sticky pear-infused syrup from his chin.

"After getting assigned or assigning himself to the board, he got a message. I never saw it, but I saw his reaction to it."

Hatch held a forkful of omelet in front of her mouth. "A threat?"

"Likely. Again, I'm basing this on his reaction, not what he said. Linden pretended as though it was nothing important. I considered chalking it up to an overzealous imagination. Us folk, who've seen a bit more than the average, tend to look at every situation through a unique lens."

"Agreed."

"He got another message this morning. Just before leaving the house to head to the parole hearing. This time there's no disputing its effect. Linden said it was an old friend." Carver grunted. "I've got old friends. Less now than before. And I definitely don't react the way he did when they reach out."

"From the sounds of it, I'm guessing he didn't talk about it with you?" Hatch asked.

"We were stuck in this car together for nearly two hours and he didn't mention a word about it. Hell, he didn't speak much at all."

"Any chance it could be a mistress threatening to put him on blast to the wife?" Banyan shrugged at Hatch.

"Linden? No way. That's something with the utmost certainty. He's a family man through and through. His whole reason for moving out of the city to his two-horse town was to give his wife and kids a better life."

"You need us to dig into this Novik guy and see if it's related. Then what?" Hatch asked.

"If there's a connection, something actionable, I'll forward it on to the proper authorities. Not looking to wage a war, just prevent one." Carver's drawl lingered. "Don't need you two putting yourselves in harm's way."

She'd found herself at the epicenter of disaster more times than she could count, most of which were never the intended course. Hatch's code forced an obligation to help those in need. The line in the sand was crossed any time good people were hurt. She was compelled to ensure those responsible were held accountable and dealt a punishment fit for the crime.

"Gotta go. Looks like Linden's finished up with the hearing. Keep me posted and I'll do the same." Carver ended the call without waiting for a response.

Banyan stabbed at the last of his pancakes. "Easy peasy."

"I thought you guys said the only easy day was yesterday?" Hatch thought of one of the SEAL mantras she'd heard Cruise recite on more than one occasion.

"Guess we better see what today has in store for us, then."

Sue appeared. "I saw you were on a call. Didn't want to bother you. How was everything?"

"Best meal I've had in a while." Hatch finished the last bite of her breakfast. She sank back into the seat cushion and let out a contented sigh.

"Anything else I can get you?"

Banyan took the final bite of the pancake. "I think that'll do it for us."

"I hope I see you in here again before you leave. Plenty more on that menu." She left the bill with a wink and cleared the plates.

Hatch pulled out her wallet and counted out the cash. She doled out an extra fifty.

"Big tipper."

"She needs it more than I do." Hatch slid out of the booth and stood. "Maybe that device of yours can do some good after all."

NINE

Chapter 9

L<small>INDEN MOVED DOWN THE CONCRETE STEPS AND HEADED FOR THE</small> Range Rover. He moved quicker than his normal ambling pace, fighting against an urge to break into a sprint. Long ago, working the streets of Phoenix as a beat cop, he'd learned that running will result in two guarantees: He'd miss relevant evidence or suspects, and he'd arrive to his destination winded. The other, less tangible byproduct was the increased panic induced by a frantic reaction to stress. The last thing he wanted to do was add any more to the overwhelming sense of dread plaguing his mind since reading the last message from the unknown sender.

Sweat flooded his dress shirt, and he tossed the suitcoat in the backseat as he entered the passenger side of the SUV. He let the air conditioner work its magic to reduce the dark blue damp circles extending out from under his armpits.

"Looks like you went swimming. Everything go okay in there?" Carver asked.

"Novik's not getting out, if that's what you mean." Linden was half-listening. His mind was running the list of potential meanings of the message. None of them good. He replayed the words Novik said to him as he was extricated from the hearing. *This will cost you in ways you've never dreamed of.*

"Then why do you look like you've seen the Reaper?"

"Maybe I have." Linden thought of his most prized possession. His family. "I've got to reach Amy."

"What is it?"

"They're coming for my family." His hand trembled uncontrollably as he fumbled with his phone and called his wife. After several rings, it went to voicemail. "Call me as soon as you get this." He then hung up and sent the same message by text. He wanted her to get the sense of urgency without throwing her into a tailspin.

Linden scrolled through his contact list until he found the main number for the school. A cheery receptionist named Cheryl answered. "This is Harvey Linden. I'm the father of Mia and Ethan Linden. I need to speak with the SRO immediately."

"Is there an issue?" Her voice was less cheery now, concern lining the edge of her words.

"Just patch me through, please."

Linden rocked in his seat, adrenaline pumping through his veins. It had taken less than thirty seconds for the secretary at the front desk to connect him with the School Resource Officer, but it felt like thirty minutes for a male voice to come through the receiver. "This is Officer Dale Goodard. How can I help you?"

"This is Harvey Linden. I need you to get my kids and move them to a safe location."

"Is there a problem?"

Linden fought the desire to scream into the phone but held back on berating the officer. It was only natural to probe. "I'm a retired Phoenix detective. I've just received a direct threat against my family, and I need to ensure that they are safe. Can you do this for me?"

"Yes. Of course." Goodard's tone changed. "Do you think there's a potential schoolwide threat?"

Linden knew the reason for the question. Lockdown drills were as commonplace as fire drills in a day and age when active shooter threats were continually on the rise. Goodard needed to know if he needed to call the cavalry. "I don't think so. These people are danger-ous, but they're not stupid."

"Okay. Good." Goodard let out a sigh of relief. "We've got a safe space. It's a windowless room used for students who need time away to destress. I'll take your children there and stay with them until I hear from you."

"Thank you." Linden felt a fraction of worry subside. "I will update you as soon as I can. The only people my children are to be released to are myself, my wife, or Max Carver, my head of security. Is that clear?"

"Absolutely. Is there anything else I can do?"

"I know this is going to be hard but try to keep my kids calm."

"Will do. To save any delay in contacting me, I'm going to give you my cell."

Linden jotted down Goodard's phone number and ended the call. He tried his wife again. No answer. His pulse quickened. "It's an hour plus drive home."

"Let's see if I can shave some time off." Carver backed out of the space and raced out of the parking lot.

Linden watched the prison fade into the backdrop. Anton Novik had been returned to the confines of his cell, but his reach extended far beyond its thick concrete walls. He hoped to be able to stop it before it touched his family.

Carver activated the tablet between them while he deftly steered around a slower moving vehicle. The display showing a live feed from the security cameras installed around the exterior of the Linden property popped up. "Good news. Your wife's car is in the driveway."

Linden exhaled. "I didn't even think to check."

"Happens to the best of us. Fear has a way of giving tunnel vision." Carver manipulated his fingers across the different camera footage, enlarging each to full screen as he did. "Looks like the coast is clear."

Linden stared down at the screen, taking time to analyze each frame and looking for anything out of the ordinary. On the backside of the house, he saw a man and his heart skipped a beat until he focused in and realized it was their gardener, Miguel.

"She's terrible about answering her phone. Always has been. Good thing we put those cameras in." Linden looked up and forced a laugh.

"Shit." Carver swerved to avoid an eighteen-wheeler cutting over into their lane. After dodging the big truck, his eyes cast back down at the screen. "You expecting a delivery?"

The thumping in his chest began again as Linden looked at the camera covering the front gate. Parked just outside was a black panel van. The tinted glass on the windshield obscured the driver from view.

An arm reached out to press the call box. Linden zoomed in. His heart sank at the sight of the tattoo extending along the inside of the driver's forearm. Black ink depicting a venomous snake with a woman's head. Linden had seen it before. He knew it well. The tattooed image of Žaža, a Belarusian mythological creature. The identifying mark of the Novik family. A moment later, the screen went black. All the cameras were now offline.

TEN

Chapter 10

AMY LINDEN TURNED ONTO THE PRIVATE DRIVEWAY LEADING TO HER home and rolled down the windows of her nearly silent Prius. As She drove slowly, the fragrant aroma of budding flowers lining the path wafted into the car. Inhaling deeply, Amy smiled, embracing the solitude and beauty of her desert oasis. She and Harvey had bought their dream house years ago, and she'd vowed never to take their good fortune for granted.

Through the wrought iron bars, she saw Miguel still hard at work. She was excited to get changed into her yardwork clothes and join him. She leaned out and punched Ethan's birthdate into the keypad, the metallic buttons heated by the sun. When the gate was first installed, she'd asked Harvey why they couldn't just get an automatic opener. He said something about the signal being easy to duplicate. He also gave her a spiel about using randomized keycodes. But after several lockouts and the calls from Amy asking him for the code, he caved and allowed her to reset it to one she could remember.

The familiar mechanical clicks and whirring sounded, and the gate slowly swung inward. She parked in the shade of the pergola, grabbed her bags from the trunk, and made her way up the wide bluestone steps, leading to the porch.

Miguel, who was diligently trimming back a mesquite tree, released his grip on his pruning shears and gave a friendly wave. "Will you be joining me today?"

"Looking forward to. Just let me set these bags down and get changed. How about I bring us out some sweet tea?"

"Sounds wonderful." Miguel tipped his hat and went back to work.

Amy headed inside. The temperature-controlled air was circulated by several large ceiling fans. She set her purse and phone on the kitchen island before taking her shopping bags upstairs to her room.

The intercom chimed just as she reached the top of the stairs, indicating that someone was at the gated entrance. Amy made her way over to the wall-mounted device which showed a live feed of the entrance. Parked at the gate was a black van with tinted windows.

Amy depressed the talk icon on the display. "Can I help you?"

"I have delivery for a Harvey Linden." The delivery driver spoke with a thick accent.

Since the advent of online delivery services like Amazon, it seemed as though they received a package a day, sometimes multiple times in the same day. She buzzed him in and headed down the hall to the bedroom.

She set the bags beside the shoe rack near the entrance to her walk-in closet. After exchanging her yoga pants for jeans, Amy made her way back downstairs to receive the delivery.

As she passed by the kitchen, her cellphone chirped, signaling a missed call. Glancing at the screen, she noticed she'd missed several. Her husband had tried to reach her. Before she could check the message, there was a knock at the front door. She made a mental note to call him back after.

The knock persisted. Amy opened the door, annoyed at both the interruption and impatience of the deliveryman. "You could've just left it on the doorstep."

The driver eyed her carefully before handing her the package. He then set a clipboard onto the top of the box. "Sign, please."

The manners of some people. She thought about lashing out

with some thoughts on the matter. After taking a second to evaluate the man standing before her, she opted for silent resistance instead. He had a look in his eyes. She'd seen it in the junkies who frequented her hospital's emergency room, a look of desperation bordering on anger. The quicker he went, the faster she could get on with her day.

"Wait here." Amy took the box and stepped inside, placing it on the kitchen island. She set the clipboard beside it and clicked the pen. Amy became aware the delivery driver had followed her inside and was now standing directly behind her.

She tried to beat down the panic rising in her chest, attributing the miscommunication to a language barrier. The attempt at rationalization was dashed when Amy felt a cloth being pressed over her mouth.

She struggled against the driver's strong grip, desperate to break free. As they grappled, Amy noticed a distinctive tattoo on the inside of the man's left forearm—a snake with a woman's head covered most of his skin. Despite her best efforts, the driver overpowered her, and Amy felt herself growing weaker as she fought to remain conscious.

In a last-ditch attempt to escape, Amy bit down hard on the cloth, tearing through it and sinking her teeth into the kidnapper's palm. The man cursed loudly, his grip loosening just enough for Amy to let out a choked scream. But the reprieve was short-lived, and the kidnapper quickly reasserted his control over her.

As darkness crept into the edges of her vision, Amy felt herself being dragged towards the front door. Sunlight came in a fractal kaleidoscope as they crossed the threshold and onto the front stoop.

A sudden blur of movement caught the corner of her eye. A glint of light reflected off a metallic object hurtling towards them. Her abductor howled. Miguel had come to her rescue. He wielded his pruning shears like a sword. The sharp blade had found their mark, slicing through the man's flesh and cutting a gash along his tattooed arm. Blood poured, a dark red separating the woman's head from the snake's body.

Amy crumpled to the ground, the effects of the chloroform finally overwhelming her. In the timeless seconds before her tunnel vision collapsed further inward, she heard a solitary gunshot ring out.

Through her hazy vision, she saw Miguel collapse beside her. Their eyes met, and in his, a deep sadness and an unspoken apology.

The kidnapper scooped her up onto his shoulder. Amy's body bounced along as she was carried down the steps to the waiting van. Her last glimpse was of her home's facade shrinking in the distance until the world faded to nothingness.

ELEVEN

Chapter 11

LINDEN NEARLY DOVE OUT OF THE VEHICLE AND SCALED THE BLACK wrought iron gate. Waiting the intolerable number of seconds it took for the gate to swing open gave his heart time to dump enough adrenaline into his bloodstream to cause his body to quiver, and enough time for his mind to play out every possible scenario. None of them good.

Worry gave way to utter panic as he sprinted from the vehicle toward the front door of his home. A dark red smear extended from the ivory white of the frame and disappeared into the stained wood, reappearing again on the brass knob.

Going against every lesson he'd ever learned regarding the entry of a crime scene and the tactics needed to address any potential unknown threat, Harvey Linden darted forward and screamed, "Amy!"

Carver was tight on his heels. Taking up alongside him, he gripped his shoulder as they reached the brick porch. His sidearm, a modified Glock 22, was held close to his chest with the barrel pointing toward the house. "Best if I take the lead here."

Linden nearly slapped his hand free. In the split-second pause Carver's interruption provided, he knew the man was right. Linden was too emotionally charged. He'd been through enough doors in his day to know the importance of clear headedness in times like this, and the deadly ramifications. Carver's experience in such matters was unquestionable. His service record served as a testimony of his skill in dealing with such threats. Linden defaulted to his top security man's judgement. He pulled out his sidearm, stacked up behind Carver, and prepared to move.

With a twist of the bloodstained knob, the door swung open. Carver entered, filling the void and breaking to the right. Linden followed behind and moved to the left. They divided the room in half and each man swept for threats, entering only deep enough to ensure it was cleared. Satisfied it was, they met in the middle.

Linden no longer called his wife's name. He'd reset his mind to the task at hand. Clear the house. Find Amy. His eyes followed the trail of blood. It disappeared around the dining area and into the kitchen.

Carver didn't speak. He signaled his intent, using his hand. He indicated that he'd follow the path of blood and directed Linden to move down the hallway and enter the kitchen from the other side. Linden nodded his understanding. Carver pressed his weapon out ahead of him and began moving forward. Linden did the same, heading down the hallway.

He couldn't help feeling the surrealness of it all. Clearing his house for a potential threat, hoping against hope that this trail of blood was not his wife's. The house felt different now, a violation changing the way he saw everything inside.

Ahead, the hallway opened into the kitchen. The stained glass rainbow his daughter had made hung from the window above the sink and splashed the tile floor in a spectrum of vibrant colors.

In the short pause he took before making his entry, he heard a faint sound. He quieted his breathing to hear it better. It was a low rumbling noise. A whimper.

Linden rushed into the room and nearly slipped on the blood splattered tile floor. Carver was closing in fast from the other side.

Both men took aim at the man on the floor. A hand, palm painted red, reached out.

A few milliseconds later, Linden recognized the crumpled form at his feet. He holstered his sidearm and knelt down beside him. He felt the warm liquid penetrate his slacks. "Miguel. Where are you hit?"

His gardener pointed to his shoulder. "Mr. Linden. I'm sorry."

The impact of Miguel's words left him speechless. A numbness washed over him in a way he'd never experienced. Linden sank back against the pantry door.

Carver took up alongside the wounded man and began evaluating the extent of the damage. "He'll live. It's a through and through. Looks like the bullet passed between the shoulder and bicep."

Carver's voice seemed distant. Linden was somewhere else now. He was buried alongside his wife. Lost in the darkness.

"Did you hear me?" Carver shook Linden's shoulders. "Get your head in the game."

Linden's head bobbled and banged into the pantry, jarring him from his lapse into despair. "What? Yes. I heard. He's gonna be okay."

"She's not dead." Carver locked eyes with Linden and kept his blood-covered hands pressed firmly against his employer's shoulders. "They took her. But she's alive. There's still a play here. We just need to figure out what it is."

Linden nodded. Carver's grip released.

"Keep pressure on his arm. I'm going to run to the car. I've got a trauma kit in there." Carver waited for a second, as if to ensure Linden got the message.

Linden pushed himself back into a kneeling position. The coldness of despair receded. He did as Carver instructed. Grabbing a wad of paper towels, he pressed firmly into his gardener's right shoulder.

Miguel winced. "I tried. I really did."

"I know. I see that. I can't thank you enough—" His words caught in his throat.

Carver returned with a black pouch the size of a fanny pack. Unzipping it, he revealed the contents. "This has everything we need to patch him up until we can get him to a hospital."

"No hospital," Miguel pleaded, his voice strained.

Linden understood Miguel's fear. When he'd hired him, Linden had known Miguel was an undocumented immigrant but had chosen to overlook it. Miguel was a hardworking man, dedicated to earning enough money to bring his family to America. Linden paid him a fair wage, and in return, Miguel worked tirelessly, never complaining.

"Can you do it?" Linden asked.

"I've worked with a lot worse." Carver rolled back his sleeve. There were two jagged scars, one on the forearm below the elbow and one above.

"You stitched that yourself?" Linden had seen the scars before, but never asked. He had some of his own. He'd always treated them like secrets, only telling their stories if and when the time was right.

"If you want it done right, sometimes you've got to do it yourself." He looked down at Miguel. "Don't worry. It's a lot easier to do on someone else."

Carver knelt beside Miguel and carefully cut away the blood-soaked shirt with trauma shears from his kit. He assessed the wound, noting the entry and exit points. "Lucky for you, it missed the bone and major vessels."

Pulling out a pack of QuikClot gauze, he tore it open. "This might sting a bit, but it'll help stop the bleeding." Carver packed the hemostatic gauze into both holes, applying firm pressure. Miguel gritted his teeth, stifling a grunt.

After a few minutes, Carver removed the gauze and inspected the wounds again. The bleeding had slowed significantly. He irrigated the wounds with a sterile saline solution, flushing out any debris.

"Looks clean." Carver reached for a suture kit. "Now I'm going to close these up. It won't be pretty, but it'll hold."

Using a pre-threaded curved needle, Carver began stitching the wounds closed with precise, efficient movements. Miguel remained stoic. He offered an occasional sharp breath, betraying his discomfort.

Finally, Carver tied off the last suture. He then applied antibiotic ointment to the wounds before covering them with sterile gauze pads and securing them in place with medical tape.

"There." He rocked back on his heels to inspect his handywork. "That'll hold. We'll need to keep an eye out for infection, but you should be good to go. A few inches in either direction and we might be having a very different conversation."

Miguel nodded gratefully. His face remained pale, but his eyes were clear. "Thank you."

"Think you can stand?" Linden asked, before helping Miguel to his feet.

Miguel balanced himself against the island while Carver went to the sink and filled a glass with water. Before he could begin asking for details, Linden's phone vibrated. He took it out and saw it was the same number who'd texted him after exiting the prison. He stepped away and read the message.

Time to meet. Come alone. No cops.

Linden waited to respond. He saw the three dots indicating another message was being typed.

Remember the old spot?

None of the messages sent prior to this gave him any idea who the sender was, aside from the fact that it had to have been someone from the Novik family's goon squad. But this last message made him think he had it all wrong. He typed his response.

Who is this?

A second later, a name popped up. A name he hadn't heard in a very long time. And one he'd hoped never to have a reason to again.

Burner.

Linden felt a renewed sense of dread take hold. He grabbed the keys to the Range Rover and started for the door.

Carver called after him. "Where you headin' off to?"

"Something I've got to do." Linden gave an apologetic look.

"If it's about Amy, I should come along."

"I have to do this one alone." Linden lingered, his gaze holding Carver's. "Do me a favor. Grab the kids. Take them somewhere safe."

Carver nodded slowly, understanding the gravity of the request. "Will do."

Linden struggled to find the right words, his thoughts jumbled. "If I—" He paused, taking a breath. "Just tell them I love 'em. You'll do that for me, okay?"

"I will." Carver looked torn, his loyalty and concern evident in his eyes. "I can help with this, whatever it is. You've just gotta let me in."

"If I could, I would." With a final nod, Linden turned and left, the weight of his decision hanging heavy on his shoulders.

His light blue shirt was now much darker. As he walked fast, he looked at the burgundy smudges added to the damp sweat stains. Linden jumped into the SUV and whipped it around the driveway, heading for the meeting location.

TWELVE

Chapter 12

Hatch and Banyan headed back to the motel, their bellies full and with a starting point for their intel gathering. At the moment, this assignment felt more like library research than the type she'd grown accustomed to. After her time in Florida, she wasn't complaining. It was a welcome change. Staying off the radar and hunkering down for a couple of days could be just what the doctor ordered to get her mind and body back in shape.

As Banyan pulled the Jeep into the motel's drive, Hatch scanned the lot. It was empty, with no sign of Ernie and his daughter. The car he'd raced off in hadn't returned. Hatch's thoughts drifted to the little girl she'd cradled in her arms.

She'd treated snake bites for fellow soldiers and once for a former lover, when her first kiss with Dalton Savage had been interrupted by a rattler. Those past experiences were nerve-racking in their own right, but children were different. An adult body was capable of fending off the effects of the venom for longer. Camila was brave, but Hatch was still haunted by the fear permeating the little girl's eyes. She closed her own and tried to push the thought from her head.

"Your place or mine," Banyan said, a playful smile on his face.

"Let's use your room. Mine's a bit of a mess right now." Earlier, after showering, Hatch had done her best to wash the blood from her t-shirt using a bar of hand soap. She then hung it over the curtain rod to dry.

Banyan unlocked the door and gave a dramatic bow as he opened it for Hatch. "And who said chivalry was dead?"

A moment later, the two were huddled around Banyan's laptop. Hatch was out of her element, watching Banyan's fingers dance across the keyboard with an almost superhuman speed. His eyes remained locked on the screen, darting back and forth as he navigated the digital pathways.

"Alright, let's see what we can find on this Novik guy. See how these dots connect to Linden," Banyan said, "but first, we need to make sure we're not leaving any digital breadcrumbs for someone else to follow."

"I'd heard about something like this from a gang instructor during my MP basic course. He said that some of the gangs, the big ones with national recognition, have their own websites. A way of trying to show the world that they're a philanthropical social club instead of a bunch of drug dealing, murderous thugs." The spice from the green chilies of her omelet continued to linger, causing her to clear her throat. "The instructor said it's typically safe to do a one-time passthrough of their site. The second time and they're looking back at you."

"Whoever taught you knew their stuff. While we might be able to get away with poking around their public-facing sites once or twice, we have to assume anything beyond that is going to raise some red flags. If we keep digging, there's a good chance they'll start digging into us." Banyan didn't look up from the display. "And when it comes to outfits like the Noviks, you have to be careful. Guys like this are no joke and they typically employ their own tech experts. Mark my words, they're always watching."

Hatch's eye narrowed on the screen. It was a series of prompts, all of it Greek to her. "And you have a way to shield us?"

Banyan leaned back in his chair, a thoughtful expression on his face. "That's why we need to be smart about this. We can't just go in guns blazing, digitally speaking. We need to use anonymizing tools, cover our tracks, and be selective about the information we access. Make sense?"

Hatch nodded. "You're driving this boat. I'm just a passenger."

He returned his focus to the opened command prompt and began typing a series of cryptic letter, number combinations. "I'm routing our connection through multiple proxies and VPNs. This will mask our IP address and make it much harder for anyone to track our online activity."

Hatch nodded again, only half understanding the technical jargon but fully appreciating Banyan's expertise.

"Now, let's dive deep," Banyan continued, his fingers still flying over the keys. "The surface web, which is what most people use daily, only makes up a small fraction of the internet. The real juicy stuff is hidden deep and to access it, we need to use a special browser called The Onion Router, or TOR."

He launched the TOR browser, and the screen filled with a complex network of nodes and pathways. "TOR encrypts our traffic and bounces it through multiple servers around the world, making it virtually impossible to trace."

Once the browser was up and running, Banyan navigated to a search engine Hatch had never seen before. "Is that what I'm looking at? This is the Dark Web?"

"To put it bluntly, yes. This is a specialized search engine designed to navigate the world beneath the world," he said. "It indexes sites and databases that aren't accessible through regular search engines like Google."

Hatch leaned in closer. She smelled the sweetness of the prickly pear syrup that was now infused with Banyan. She watched as he entered a series of keywords related to Novik and Linden. A few seconds later, the search engine returned a list of results. Hatch quickly scanned through them.

"Okay, here's something interesting." He clicked on a link. "Appears as though there was some controversy surrounding Linden's arrest of Novik. Some people claimed that the evidence against him was planted. It was dismissed during the trial and was grounds for an appeal that was later denied."

Hatch studied the screen. "Does it give any details? Or say anything about who might have planted the evidence?"

Banyan shook his head. "No, but it does mention that Linden retired shortly after the arrest."

"You think Carver's employer might not be the white knight he claims to be?"

"Wouldn't be the first time the lines between good and evil were crossed." Banyan intertwined his fingers and cracked his knuckles. "And what's the root of all evil?"

"Love of money," Hatch said under her breath. "Linden might have framed Novik, taken his cut, and then used his money to start a new business?"

"Anything's possible. But we need more evidence to prove it. Let me see what else I can dig up."

He continued to search, using advanced operators and filtering techniques to narrow down the results. Hatch watched in amazement as he navigated through the digital underworld with ease, uncovering bits and pieces of information that slowly began to form a picture.

Over an hour had ticked by, and Banyan continued his pursuit down the digital catacombs. None of their findings shed any additional light on the case in question and their connection. However, it did highlight some of Linden's history as a police officer. Aside from the claim made by Anton Novik, he was a decorated cop, receiving numerous citations for bravery.

"Maybe it was personal." Hatch was half speaking to herself.

"How do you mean?"

She tapped the article on the screen. "Says here that Linden took a bullet. What if he didn't go after Novik for monetary purposes?"

"Vengeance can drive people to do things they'd otherwise never consider."

Hatch knew the truth in those words better than most, having spent considerable time avenging wrongs. She'd taken aim at the people responsible for her father's death. And she'd taken up arms to serve as the archangel for those who were incapable of doing so themselves.

"There's got to be something we're missing. Doesn't add up," Hatch muttered, frustration edging into her voice. "Criminals get arrested all the time, but they rarely go after the investigator who brought them down. Sure, they might hold a grudge, but targeting them? The blowback would be insane. We need to run this by Carver and see what he thinks of it all."

As if on cue, Banyan's phone buzzed. He glanced at the screen. "Speak of the devil."

Hatch leaned in as Banyan answered and put the call on speaker. Carver's voice filled the room, tense and urgent. "Linden's wife has been abducted."

Carver spent the next several minutes filling them in. It took a moment to process the dramatic shift from the benign nature of their web-based intelligence gathering to the current state of things. Hatch organized the information in her head. All things pointed at the Novik family. Hatch knew time was of the essence, especially in a hostage situation. She felt the clock beginning to tick and that all too familiar urge to do something about it.

"Did you call the police?" Hatch asked.

"Linden left after receiving another message. He said not to involve law enforcement or they'll kill her."

Banyan's jaw tightened. "And you have proof-positive it's the Noviks?"

"Didn't get a visual on the guy in the van, but Linden said the tattoo, a snake with a woman's head, is proof enough."

Hatch and Banyan exchanged grim looks.

Carver continued. "The kids are safe at the school. I'm going to pick them up and take them somewhere secure."

An idea sparked in Hatch's mind. "Bring them to our room at the Jumping Cholla. Besides us, it's vacant. And definitely off the radar. They can lie low there until we get a handle on this."

"Good plan," Carver agreed. "I'm sending you a link to the GPS tracker on Linden's Range Rover. Looks like he's heading toward Phoenix."

Banyan pulled up the tracker on his phone, studying the map. "Got it. We're on our way."

As they gathered their gear, Banyan's phone alerted. The GPS pinged the vehicle had changed speeds, slowing as it neared the town of Apache Junction.

Hatch left a note for Ernesto. Figuring it best that Carver and the children remain incognito, she said she had a friend who would be stopping by for a visit with two children and asked if he could give them the key to Banyan's room. She left enough money to cover an extra room.

She stepped out into the midday sun. Banyan pulled the car up and Hatch hopped into the passenger side.

Banyan accelerated away from the motel. "Looks like this is turning into a little more than the fact-finding mission we'd originally been tasked with."

"Guess we're going to find out." Hatch felt a strange sense of calm at the prospect. Looming threats and high stakes had become her baseline, a byproduct of nature and nurture. She felt her mind and body preparing for the unknown.

THIRTEEN

Chapter 13

LINDEN SAT IN THE RANGE ROVER. THE AIR CONTINUED TO BLOW
through the vents but did little to fight against the beads of sweat
dotting his forehead. His body was overheating as each passing
minute fueled his panic. He arrived at the designated meeting location
nearly a half hour ago. He'd been instructed to wait until he received
another message. There had been none.

Linden's cop senses were on high alert as he scanned the Rusty
Spur's parking lot for any sign of Novik's crew. The remote bar's lot
was sparsely filled, which wasn't surprising given the early hour. The
few cars and motorcycles scattered around likely belonged to day
drinkers. Linden had chosen this location for its distance from the
city and limited number of patrons, making it one of his go-to spots
for meeting informants like Burner.

It struck Linden as odd that Burner had directed him here now,
considering their history. The fact that Burner selected the place
they'd met to discuss the plan to takedown Anton was unsettling, and
the implications made him uncomfortable. Whoever had put Burner
up to this knew more about Linden than he liked.

The waiting period gave Linden a chance to slow down, weigh his options, and plan his next move. He considered reaching out to some trusted friends still on the force, calling in a favor or two, but the message had been clear about involving law enforcement. Linden was confident, though he could never prove it, that some of his former coworkers were on the take. Too many cases had slipped through his fingers for him to believe otherwise. He couldn't risk it.

Every plan led to the same outcome: his wife dead. The only chance was to stay the course, play their game, and wait for the right moment to make his move. A beat-up, rust-colored Toyota entered the lot and slowly made its way to a spot in the far corner, parking beside a desert willow. The combination of the tree's shade and the car's darkly tinted windows made it nearly impossible to identify the driver.

Linden stared intently at the Toyota, making no effort to hide his concentration, as if squinting would grant him the superhuman ability to pierce the dark barrier of the tinted windows. The sudden buzzing of his cellphone, rattling against the loose change in the cupholder, jarred him from his focus. The incoming message was from Burner.

Go inside. Get a table in the back.

Rage swelled within him. Part of Linden wanted to ram his SUV into the smaller sedan and beat the truth out of Burner right then and there. He fought to control himself, taking several deep breaths of the cool air blowing against his face. Linden reminded himself to play their game. He'd find a way to save Amy, or he'd die trying.

Linden untucked his shirt, covering his pistol tucked into his waistband before stepping from the Range Rover. Dirt kicked up from the ground as he walked across the lot toward the bar's entrance. He fought the urge to give a side glance at the red car idling to his right. Each step forward was one step closer to getting her back.

The weathered wooden exterior and flickering neon sign gave the impression of a place that had seen its fair share of history. The doors were cut to look like saloons of the past. He pushed through.

Linden stood in the threshold for a moment, giving time for his eyes to adjust to the darkness. He'd exchanged the dry warm air outside for the stale beer-infused bar interior. No one bothered to look up from their drinks as he stepped deeper inside. Of the six patrons stretched across the bar stools, half looked as though they'd already hit their daily limit. One man hugged his mug with both hands while propping himself upright with the wooden pillar.

Seeing the slovenly bunch, he was reminded why this place had been ideal for meeting with those who wished to maintain their anonymity. He could probably pull off an armed robbery without any of these guys being able to give a description.

The bartender was the only one to pay him any mind. He was a barrel-chested man with a dark tattoo stretching up the left side of his neck, disappearing beneath a thick black beard before reappearing again behind his ear and along his bald head. He gave Linden a slight nod of acknowledgement before going about topping off one of the mugs in front of him.

Linden did as the message instructed and found a seat at a table located towards the back of the bar. He positioned himself to face the door. He moved his hand to his gun. Linden scanned the room until he was confident no one was paying attention to him. Satisfied, he removed the pistol from his waist and tucked it under his thigh.

The bartender stepped out from behind the bar and walked over to the table. His voice was as gruff as his exterior. "What's your poison?"

"Waiting on somebody." Linden kept one eye on the door.

"You know where to find me." The bartender grumbled something under his breath as he made his way back to the bar.

A beam of bright light cut a line through the gloom. The sun temporarily cast the man at the doorway in silhouette. He stood there, just as Linden had, before closing himself to the darkness.

Linden's fingers were already dancing along the textured grip of his pistol. He felt like he'd been transported back to the Wild West, a gunslinger preparing for the showdown.

Linden's eyes narrowed as he studied the familiar face staring at him from across the room. The man had aged since their last encounter, his once youthful features now weathered and worn. Linden tensed, watching as his former informant, Burner, approached and took a seat across from him.

"Been a while," Burner said, his voice low and strained.

Linden leaned forward, his elbows on the table. "Never thought I'd see you again, especially not like this." He studied Burner's face, noting the nervous tic as he rubbed his hands together.

"Wish it wasn't under these circumstances," Burner replied, avoiding Linden's gaze.

Questions swirled in Linden's mind, but one pushed its way to the forefront. "Where's Amy?" he demanded, his tone a mix of desperation and barely contained anger.

"She's safe." He looked around the room. His eyes betrayed the panic within. "As long as you do what they say."

Linden felt an overwhelming fear creep up the back of his neck. He moved his hand away from the gun. Seeing Burner confirmed two things: the Noviks were responsible, and they knew the truth about Anton's arrest. What that meant for Linden was unknown, but there was no way it would end well.

FOURTEEN

Chapter 14

HATCH AND BANYAN ARRIVED AT THE RUSTY SPUR SALOON, A WATERING
hole outside of Apache Junction, about forty-five minutes after
Linden. The GPS tracker confirmed his vehicle was still parked in the
lot. Opting for a covert approach, Hatch guided their vehicle to an
abandoned gas station across the street, close enough to maintain a
clear view of Linden's SUV, but far enough to avoid drawing attention
from any potential counter-surveillance.

The Rusty Spur Saloon was a throwback, a blend of the old west
with a hint of a hardcore biker element. Hatch's experience in navigating these types of establishments had taught her to recognize the
inherent dangers they presented. The remote location and rough-
around-the-edges atmosphere made it a fitting choice for Linden's
secretive meeting.

Linden's Range Rover was parked near a dumpster in the back of
the lot. Hatch noted the retired cop's situational awareness. Never put
your back to potential threats. In this case, his tactic was definitely
warranted.

"Looks like he's been here nearly forty-five minutes." Banyan examined the tracker's time stamp.

"I guess we should take a peek at who's calling the shots." Hatch released her seatbelt and adjusted the compact semi-automatic Glock, centering it at the small of her back to limit the weapon's profile.

"Think going inside is a good idea?"

"Nobody knows who we are. Linden doesn't even know we're working on his behalf."

"Yeah, I get it. That's not what worries me." Banyan scanned the lot. "Look at this place. It's definitely a shithead bar. Likely it'll be filled with a bunch of regulars at this time of day."

"Are you saying I don't look the part?"

"Neither of us do. This doesn't look like it has much of a lunch crowd. Regardless of whether Linden knows who we are, he'd definitely know we don't belong."

Hatch mulled this over. Banyan was right. Any cop worth his salt would immediately pick up on someone out of place. That doubles for criminals. "So, what, we just wait?"

"Not exactly." Banyan reached into the back seat. He retrieved his laptop and set it between them, resting it on the center console. "We may not be able to see inside, but we can hear."

A few seconds later, he accessed the Omnisphere app. Overlapping voices filled the air. Hatch was reliving that same disorientation she experienced while in the diner. "How are we going to isolate Linden's conversation?"

"My guess, it'll be the guys not slurring." A couple keystrokes later, the voices began dropping off one by one. A conversation, spoken in hushed tones, was all that was left. "Bingo."

LINDEN TOOK a moment to collect his thoughts. The bartender arrived with two pints. He paid cash, leaving enough for a tip and ensuring the bartender had no reason to return. Linden took a sip of the cold beer. It felt good going down, but he had no intention of finishing the drink in hand. He only drank it to justify his presence in the establishment.

Burner lifted the mug and consumed nearly half of it before setting it back on the table in front of him. His hands shook. "I never meant for this to happen."

"Then how did it?" Linden looked at the bruising under his left eye and the small cut on his upper lip that accompanied the greasy hair and disheveled state of his clothes. He chose his next words wisely. "You using again?"

"No." Burner looked hurt by the comment. "I've been clean for nearly eighteen months."

"You don't look clean."

"Screw you!" Burner's lips turned up in a snarl. "I'm not on the shit anymore. Don't believe me? Take a look." He rolled up his sleeves and turned his forearms out.

Linden looked at the old tracks, a constellation of scars winding up the pale skin. No new injection marks. "Sorry. You just seemed... off."

"Yeah? Well, you don't look so hot yourself."

"Fair." Linden ran his finger along the cool mug, cutting a line through rapidly forming condensation. "How are you involved in all of this? What's the play?"

"I'm involved because you involved me."

"That's not what I meant."

Burner cast his eyes down. "I know."

"What happened to the plan?" Linden needed to get to the bottom of this. He also read the frazzled state of his former informant, and knew that pushing too hard, too fast might cause him to shut down. He proceeded with caution. "How'd they get to you?"

"I did what you said. Really did leave it all behind. I got clean. Stayed clean. Got a job at a local juice factory. Not great but I've just been promoted to assistant manager. I even got a girl. Not from that world. A good girl, from a good family. Her name's—" Burner swallowed his words.

"Easy. The more you tell me, the more I can help."

"You can't help. No one can." A tear streamed down his cheek. He quickly wiped it away with his sleeve and took a swig of his beer. "They've got her. They've got my Jenny. Just like they got your wife."

Linden was a whirlwind of emotion. Part of him wanted to reach across the table and squeeze every detail from the man. Another part wanted to curl into a ball and scream. He saw the same desperation reflected in Burner's eyes.

"They snatched me after work a little over two weeks ago. Never saw it coming. When I woke up, I was in some kind of cell." Burner absently ran his tongue across his split lip, wincing at the pain. "I knew it was bad. Figured they'd finally put two and two together and were coming to collect."

"Why'd they let you go?"

"They didn't set me free. They have my girlfriend. And they're going to kill her." Burner's voice broke as another wave of sadness threatened to overwhelm him. "They told me that all I had to do was to convince you to do what they said."

"Release Anton? Are you kidding me? If you think me signing off on his parole was going to change anything, then you've forgotten how they do business."

"You think I forgot? I've spent every waking minute looking over my shoulder. You're the one who ran off to the suburbs and hid. Maybe you're the one who forgot their reach."

"They're the ones who got me assigned to oversee the hearing?"

Burner gave a mocking thumbs up. "You didn't find that odd?"

"I did. But figured I could make sure he never gets out."

"They wanted to force your hand. Expose you. Destroy you." Burner was angry again. "But you didn't play ball. Couldn't take the hint. Couldn't take a dive. No, you had to be the hero."

At the moment, Linden felt he was anything but. "I did what I thought was right."

"What you did is sign our death warrants."

"They were signed the day we took down Anton." Linden dismissed the would've, could've, should've of his past actions. He focused on the here and now. "Now what?"

"They want what they've wanted from the start. They want Anton back."

Linden threw his hands up. "It's too late. I already sent in his remand. It's an electronic submission. Nothing I can do. I can't call to order a special review board to override my decision. Plus, that would look insane. Nobody would believe that I had a sudden change of heart."

"These are not people who accept excuses. If you can't make this happen, my girlfriend and your wife will be dead. Then we'd be next. And don't think they would stop there."

Linden didn't need Burner to finish his thoughts. He knew the level of depravity the Noviks were capable of, and the depths they'd go to seek their revenge. He thought of his children and hoped that Carver was worth every penny. "Tell me about this cell they kept you in."

"What are you thinking? You're going to call the cavalry and swoop in for the rescue?"

"Sitting here and doing nothing doesn't seem like much of an alternative." Linden ran the scenario through his head. "Maybe I can buy us some time. Enough that we might be able to come up with a plan."

"Look where your last plan got us."

Linden clenched his jaw, pushing down his frustration. "Tell me about the cell. Do you think that's where they're keeping Amy?"

"I don't know what to tell you. They drugged me and threw a hood over my head. Next thing I knew, I woke up in this jail cell."

"You keep saying 'jail cell.'"

"Because that's what it was." Burner let his frustration show. "It was a jail, but not modern. It was old. I mean, really old. And it was underground."

Linden leaned forward, his interest piqued. "If you woke up inside of it, how would you know it was underground?"

"Because it was built into the rock, like a cave."

"Or more likely, a mine," Linden suggested.

"Yeah. That's how I'd describe it."

"I think I know where they're keeping them." Linden felt hopeful for the first time since his wife had been taken. "I'm going to need you to stall. Tell them I'm working on changing the parole recommendation and that I have to call in some favors. That should buy us some time."

"Time for what?"

"A rescue."

"Do you think you can pull this off?" Burner finished the rest of his beer.

"I don't see an alternative."

Linden remained seated while Burner took his leave, not wanting them to be seen walking out together. He waited until the bartender and other patrons were preoccupied before sliding his pistol out from under his thigh and returning it to his waist. Taking a moment to adjust his untucked shirt, Linden ensured the weapon was concealed from view. He sipped his beer, waiting an additional five minutes before getting up himself.

Stepping outside, Linden blinked as his eyes adjusted to the brightness. Glancing towards the spot where the red Toyota had been parked, it was gone. The branches of the willow tree shifted gently in the light breeze. As Linden made his way to his Range Rover, he noticed a blue Jeep pulling into the lot and parking in the spot next to his vehicle. The Jeep was occupied by a male driver and a female passenger.

As Linden approached his Range Rover, he couldn't shake the feeling that he was being watched. His instincts, honed by years on the force, told him to be on guard. He kept his pace steady, not wanting to alert any potential threats to his heightened state of awareness.

When he reached the driver's side door of his SUV, the window of the blue Jeep beside him began to lower. Linden's hand instinctively slid beneath his shirt, his fingers wrapping around the grip of his concealed gun. His heart raced as he prepared for the worst, his mind running through countless scenarios.

The male driver leaned slightly out of the window, his voice low and urgent. "Harvey Linden, we're friends of Max Carver, and we're here to help."

Linden paused, his hand still resting on his gun. The mention of Max Carver's name gave him reason to hesitate. Carver was one of the few people he trusted implicitly, but the unexpected appearance of these supposed allies set him on edge. He knew he had to be cautious, especially with so much at stake.

The female passenger, seeming to sense Linden's hesitation, spoke up. "We know about your wife, and we have information that could help you find her. Please, let us assist you."

Linden's mind raced as he weighed his options. Could he trust these strangers? Did he have a choice? With every passing minute, the chances of finding Amy alive grew slimmer. He knew he needed all the help he could get, but the risk of walking into a trap was ever-present.

Taking a deep breath, Linden made his decision. He slowly removed his hand from his gun and nodded towards the Jeep. "Alright, let's talk. But not here. Follow me."

As he climbed into his Range Rover, Linden couldn't shake the feeling that he was about to embark on a dangerous journey, one that would test his limits and force him to confront his deepest fears. But for Amy's sake, he was willing to do whatever it took, even if it meant putting his trust in two complete strangers.

FIFTEEN

Chapter 15

HATCH AND BANYAN FOLLOWED LINDEN'S RANGE ROVER AS HE LED
them away from the Rusty Spur Saloon. After a short drive of about
seven minutes, Linden turned onto a dusty, unmarked road that
snaked through the desert landscape. Another three minutes passed
before he brought his vehicle to a stop in a small, secluded clearing,
far from prying eyes.

As Linden exited his SUV and approached their Jeep, Hatch turned
to face their guest, who slid into the backseat. She'd noticed his right
hand had been floating close to his hip before Banyan introduced
himself, and it stayed there as he made his way into the vehicle. "Mr.
Linden, we are not a threat. Please, there's no need to consider pulling
your gun."

A flush of red crept up Linden's cheeks as he realized he'd been
caught. Bringing his hand forward, he rested it on his thigh, his
posture relaxing slightly. "You're friends of Carver?"

"More like we have a mutual friend," Hatch clarified. "Regardless,
we're here to help with your current situation."

Linden's gaze sharpened, his eyes searching Hatch's face for any sign of deception. "And what exactly do you know about my current situation?"

Hatch could see Linden remained guarded, playing the detective role and only giving enough without really giving anything at all. "We know the Novik family was trying to press you into releasing Anton Novik on parole for a case you made against him. We know you refused to be coerced into doing so, and thus they kidnapped your wife as a means of leveraging you to revise your parole denial. Anything we're missing?"

Linden flustered, his eyes wild and his breathing heavy. "How do you know all of this?"

"Carver became concerned. He called in a favor from an old friend. We are here to make sure that debt is paid."

Linden gave a slow nod. His face did little to bely the additional questions he wanted to ask. Instead, he added, "I'm going to get my wife back."

"And how do you suppose you do that?"

"I—I'm not sure. I'm still working on that."

"We understand you bought yourself a little time. That's good," Hatch said. "Let's make sure we use it wisely."

"How did you know that? Was he wearing a wire?"

Hatch glanced at Banyan before responding. "We have our methods. Your friend back there? How is he connected to the Noviks?"

Linden paused, weighing his words. "His name is Michael Flatts, better known on the streets as Burner. He was one of my informants when I was trying to take down Anton Novik. He played a crucial role in that investigation."

Hatch nodded, piecing together the information. "And now it seems he's caught up in this mess, with his girlfriend being used as leverage. But that doesn't change the fact that if we don't act quickly, they'll kill your wife."

"You're right," Linden admitted, his shoulders sagging under the weight of the situation. "When Burner mentioned the place they held him, the location he believes his girlfriend and my wife are being kept, it sounded familiar."

"Familiar how?" Hatch pressed.

"It's just a hunch, but it might be connected to the Noviks' old operations."

"It's more than we had before," Hatch pointed out. "Your history with the Novik family, your attempts to bring them down... we've done our research."

Linden chuckled dryly. "I figured as much. But there's more to the story than what's in the official records."

Banyan leaned forward, his curiosity piqued. "We suspected there might be, especially regarding the circumstances that led to Anton's arrest."

Linden took a deep breath before continuing. "I worked with several informants over the years, one of whom you just saw. Heard talk of a place they'd take people when they wanted information. In all my searching, I never found it. But today, I realized I'd been looking in the wrong area, focusing in and around Phoenix."

"Then where should you have been looking?" Hatch asked.

"Clifton. Just shy of three hours southeast of here."

"And you're certain that's the place?"

"Best guess. I went there on a field trip in high school. Clifton's an old mining town. There was a jail built into the rock. They used it for miners who got themselves into trouble. It became a bit of a tourist attraction." Linden paused thoughtfully. "I was going to take the kids last year, but when I looked it up, I saw it was under renovation."

Banyan quickly searched for the Clifton Jail on his laptop. Linden was right; it was under renovation. Digging a little deeper, Banyan looked up and asked, "Ever heard of Belaya Rus Enterprises?"

Linden sank into his seat. "It's one of the shell companies the Noviks used to give the appearance of being legitimate business owners. How did I miss that?"

Banyan shrugged. "Who would bother looking into who's behind the restoration?"

"We need a plan." Hatch turned to Banyan. "We've got to put eyes on that jail. We also need a failsafe."

Linden interrupted from the backseat, "How can I help?"

"When you were talking to your informant friend in there, you said there was no way you could change your parole decision. Is that true?" Hatch asked.

"Yes. It's an electronic submission system. As soon as the hearing concludes, I send along my recommendation for denial."

"But you said you would try to call in a favor. Is that something that could be done? Is there someone in your circle who could rescind your denial?"

"No. But I figured the Novik crew wouldn't know any better. I wanted to buy enough time to get to my wife."

Hatch glanced at the laptop, deep in thought. "If it's an electronic submission, do you think you could find your way in and work your magic?"

Banyan shrugged. "As long as I have his login credentials, I should be able to find a backdoor."

Linden's eyes went wide. "Are you two talking about hacking into a statewide law enforcement database?"

"We're going to need a failsafe," Banyan said. "If we're unable to find a way to safely rescue your wife, we'll need to have an alternative."

"You're not talking about actually releasing Anton Novik, are you?"

"If it means getting your wife back, yes. I hope it doesn't come to that, but making an exchange might be the surefire way."

"He'll never stop. You know that, right? Even if we do make the swap, he'll come again. And keep coming until my family is destroyed."

"Let's deal with the problem at hand. We'll figure out the next bridge when we cross it." Banyan closed his laptop.

"We're going to have to divide and conquer." Hatch spoke directly to Banyan. "Go with Mr. Linden in his Range Rover to the motel so that he can be with his children. I'll take your Jeep and head down to Clifton to get a recon of this jail. We've got to verify proof of life before we make a move."

Linden turned to Hatch, pleading desperation in his voice. "Let me go with you. I can help."

"No," Hatch replied firmly. "Stay with Banyan. He's going to need you to access the database and walk him through the process. Plus, you should be nearby in case your informant friend needs to meet again."

"But you're—"

"A woman?" Hatch raised an eyebrow, giving him an incredulous look.

"I was going to say you're only one person," Linden clarified. "They have an entire army. They'll kill you in a heartbeat."

Banyan chuckled. "Mr. Linden, you have no idea what this one person is capable of."

With that, the decision was made. Hatch would take Banyan's Jeep, while Linden and Banyan would return to the motel in Linden's Range Rover to link up with Carver and the kids.

After the men exited the Jeep, Hatch pulled out of the dirt lot and headed east on US 60. Not sure how much time Linden's ruse would buy them, she hoped it would be enough as she pressed down on the accelerator.

A swirl of dust kicked up, seemingly racing alongside her. What had started as a simple intelligence gathering mission had now escalated, the stakes rising with each passing moment. Hatch knew she had to rise to meet them, her determination unwavering as she sped towards Clifton.

SIXTEEN

Chapter 16

AMY LINDEN WAS JOSTLED AWAKE, HER EYES SNAPPING OPEN TO darkness. An earthy smell, reminiscent of damp soil, filled her nostrils. A rough fabric covered her face, and as she reached for it, she felt the sharp bite of plastic digging into her wrists.

Memories came in disjointed bursts, like fragments of a television show played out of order. Her breathing quickened, and she felt the familiar grip of a panic attack taking hold. Ever since a childhood incident where she'd fallen between two rocks during a birthday rock-climbing trip, Amy had struggled with a deep-rooted fear of enclosed spaces. It had taken several hours to extricate her from the tight confines, and the experience had left an indelible mark on her psyche. Countless therapy sessions well into adulthood had helped her manage her claustrophobia, but the present circumstances were putting her hard-won coping mechanisms to the test.

She closed her eyes, focusing on the calming techniques she'd practiced countless times. Inhale, two, three, four. Hold for seven. Release for eight. Amy repeated the cycle, each measured breath a small victory against the rising tide of panic. A minute passed before she felt the tension in her chest begin to ease, the vise-like grip on her lungs loosening ever so slightly.

With determined fingers, Amy worked her hands up to her face and tugged at the bag covering her head. A drawstring caught under her chin, and she blindly felt around her throat until she found the knot. It took her another minute or two of fumbling before she was able to release it and pull the hood from her face.

As the burlap potato sack fell to the plastic corrugated flooring, the earthiness of the smell made sense to her. She was in a van, that much was clear. Despite the absence of light, her vision had adapted enough to the darkness, allowing her to get a sense of her surroundings.

Her ankles were bound in a similar fashion to her wrists, white plastic zip ties tightly fitted, leaving no room to wiggle free.

Amy tried to piece together the events leading up to this moment, but it was like attempting to complete a jigsaw puzzle with missing pieces. She remembered going shopping and returning home. There was something about a delivery, but what happened next was a blur. Fragmented images flashed through her mind: her gardener, Miguel, another man whose face she couldn't quite make out, a struggle, and then a gunshot.

Her body trembled at the thought, a chill running down her spine. Still fighting through the mental fog, Amy detected a lingering taste in the back of her throat. She recalled a sweet, pungent odor and a burning sensation in her nose and throat. The man had pressed a cloth against her face, likely using chloroform to subdue her. It would account for the haze that still clouded her mind.

The van's engine rumbled, the vibrations resonating through the floorboard and into the bench where she sat. The movement, combined with the lingering effects of the drug, caused her stomach to lurch, but she fought back the urge to vomit, determined to maintain what little control she had over her body.

There was no accounting for time. Depending on the dosage, she could've been out for minutes to hours. Amy pressed the palm of her hands to the wall of the windowless side panel of the van. It was cool to the touch. She knew that it had to be much later. The desert sun was no longer at full strength.

With that realization, Amy swallowed down her fear. How far from home was she? And how would anyone ever find her? She was that little girl all over again. Trapped. Waiting for a rescue that may not be coming. The vice grip clutched her chest again and squeezed tighter than before.

She was nearly tossed from the bench to the floorboard. The vehicle had turned, swerving to the right. The engine grew quieter. The rumble was less noticeable. The van was slowing. A few minutes later, it came to a complete stop.

The engine shut off, and Amy heard the driver's door open and close. A man's voice reached her ears, speaking to another in a dialect she couldn't quite make out. The voices grew louder as the men approached the back of the van.

Quickly, she reached down and slipped the hood back over her head, plunging herself into darkness once more. The burlap scratched at her skin, its earthy scent filling her nostrils. Amy lay back on the bench, feigning unconsciousness.

The doors swung open, and a man entered. His heavy footsteps caused the van to bounce with each step. Through the ambient light filtering through the hood, she saw his dark, featureless silhouette loom over her.

Moments later, Amy was roughly hoisted from the van and slung over the man's shoulder like a sack of potatoes. As she bounced along, she peered through the bottom of the hood, searching for any clues to her whereabouts. But all she could see was dry, barren dirt.

A loud clang echoed, and the air shifted, growing cooler and damper as she was carried deeper into a new environment. A shrill creak of metal pierced the silence.

Suddenly, Amy was falling. Without warning, her captor had dropped her. Instinctively, she tried to extend her hands to break her fall, but stopped, not wanting him to know she was awake. All she could do was wait for the impact. The shockwave of pain reverberated through her bones as she hit the ground. She remained motionless, continuing her ruse of unconsciousness. The last thing she needed was another dose of chloroform; she had to stay as clear-headed as possible.

The man tugged at her bindings. She felt the cool steel of the blade graze her skin as it worked to cut her free. The newfound freedom in her hands provided a glimmer of hope. He muttered something in his native tongue, his tone harsh and derogatory. He spat on the ground near her head before his footsteps retreated. The same loud creaking sounded again, followed by a metallic clang and the distinct turn of a key.

The cold, damp concrete floor seeped into her skin, helping to counter some of the lingering nausea. Amy savored the sensation of her unbound wrists, the absence of the plastic restraints a small comfort in her dire situation.

Amy listened intently as his footsteps faded away, but she forced herself to remain still for several minutes longer. When she was certain he was gone, she slowly edged her hands up to her head and tugged off the burlap hood. Blinking in the dim light, Amy took in her surroundings, her heart pounding as she tried to make sense of her new prison.

Amy found herself in a cell unlike any she had ever seen before. The jail was built directly into the natural rock formation, the ancient bars appearing to be at least two centuries old.

As she approached the cell door to test the integrity of its lock, a noise from behind startled her. Spinning around, Amy heard a low whimper emanating from a dark corner of the cell. She squinted, her heart racing at the thought that this madman might have caged her with some feral animal.

But she was not alone. Huddled in the corner was a young woman, her eyes vacant and haunted. As Amy's vision adjusted to the dim light, she realized the woman was staring directly at her.

Slowly, the young woman scooted forward, her eyes narrowing as she scanned Amy from head to toe, as if trying to verify that she was indeed real and not some figment of her imagination. With a hoarse cough, the woman cleared her throat and spoke, her voice barely above a whisper. "We're never getting out of here."

The words struck a chord within Amy, echoing the same hopeless thoughts she had harbored all those years ago when she was trapped between the rocks. But she had been proven wrong then, and now, even in the face of this dire situation, she clung to the hope that history would repeat itself, and they would find a way to escape this nightmarish prison.

SEVENTEEN

Chapter 17

Hatch had started her journey on US 60 but had since turned onto US 191, identified as its original name by the signs lining the highway: the Coronado Trail. She'd seen her first sign for Clifton about a mile back and was closing in on her destination. Even with potential threats looming and the uncertainty of her present circumstance, she found herself drawn to the breathtaking scenery of eastern Arizona. Experience had taught her that even in chaos, beauty existed. It was often in those desperate times, when things were at their bleakest, that solace presented itself in the simplest of pleasures.

The winding road, named after the Spanish explorer Francisco Vázquez de Coronado, showcased the ruggedness of the Apache-Sitgreaves National Forest and the Blue Range Primitive Area. Just north of Clifton, the road twisted and turned. The lowering sun bounced its colorful display off the Blue River, setting the brown earth ablaze with hues of red and orange.

Dramatic elevation changes and steep grades forced her to reduce speed as she navigated the challenging stretch of roadway leading her through the surrounding mountains of the San Francisco River Valley.

The sheer drop-offs demanded her full attention and skill behind the wheel. The tight hairpin turns, some lacking guardrails, served as a reminder of the unforgiving nature of the mountain landscape.

Approximately five miles north of Clifton, Hatch reached the highest elevation of the route, where the road's challenges intensified. Along the Coronado Trail Switchbacks, danger signs posted warnings of swerving roads and steep inclines.

Twenty minutes later, Hatch was greeted by a weathered sign with the town's slogan: "The Town Too Tough To Die." The gas gauge on her car dipped towards empty, prompting Hatch to pull into a local gas station. She couldn't affect much of a rescue if her getaway car ran out of gas.

She stepped out of the car. A whistle sounded as a breeze swept through the surrounding high ground. Hatch took a moment to stretch her legs before sticking the nozzle into her tank. An older gentleman in a faded denim jacket exited the attendant's station and approached her. His sun-weathered face and calloused hands spoke of a lifetime spent in this rugged corner of Arizona.

"Welcome to Clifton." He offered a tip of his oil-stained baseball cap.

"Evening." Hatch reached for her wallet. "I was just about to head in to pay."

The attendant took a moment, his eyes scanning Hatch and then moving to the car she drove. "Guessing you're not from around here."

Hatch didn't register any judgment in the man's comment. "Just doing a little sightseeing."

The attendant looked up, as if the answer to the question was to be found in the sky above. "Here in Clifton?"

"A friend of mine told me about the jail, said it was built into the side of the mountain. Thought it might be worth checking out."

"Seems as though your friend is operating off some old information." He took a rag from his back pocket and dabbed it along the back of his neck. "Jail's under renovation. Has been for some time."

Hatch feigned disappointment. "I'd still like to take a peek, even if I can't go in."

The old man raised an eyebrow, a skeptical expression crossing his face. He seemed to be weighing the plausibility of Hatch's story, wondering why anyone would drive all the way out here just to look at a closed jail, especially with the sun setting. After a moment, he seemed to decide against probing further, shaking his head slightly.

Hatch noticed his reaction but maintained her composed demeanor, offering a friendly smile.

"Well," the attendant said, shifting his focus back to the task at hand, "best get you fueled up and on your way before it's too dark."

Hatch handed him forty dollars for the gas. The man stuck it in the breast pocket of his jacket. "Pump's already on. Just lift that handle there. I'll grab you the change when you're topped off."

"Keep it," Hatch replied, her tone casual but firm.

"Thank you." He turned halfway and stopped. "Shame you not getting to see the whole thing. Used to be a real big tourist draw 'round here." The man's expression shifted, a hint of disappointment clouding his features. "I actually used to be a tour guide there for years, back before they decided to do this big renovation."

"Was it in bad shape?"

The attendant shook his head. "I didn't think so. Jail was just fine the way it was. Hell, it was in the same condition it had been for as long as I can remember. But someone got a wild hair and decided it needed to be spruced up."

"You said it's been under renovation for a couple years?"

"That's the thing of it. I can't imagine any amount of work that would amount to three years. You hear stories."

"What kind?"

"The ones told in small towns like this when people don't have anything better to do." He ran his fingers across the stubble on his chin. "Who knows? I will say there's some odd comin's and goin's out there."

"How do you mean?"

"They keep odd hours. Every construction company I've ever known did their work during daytime. But not this crew."

"You think it's something illegal?"

"I'm no gossip. I don't like to speak on things I don't know. But I will say it wouldn't hurt to be on your toes out there."

The pump handle clicked, indicating the tank was full. Hatch looked at the price gauge. Five dollars under the payment she'd given. Five dollars well spent. "I noticed my GPS wasn't working so well for the last ten miles or so. I could use some directions."

The man chuckled. "Yeah, cell reception's spotty in these parts. Nature of the beast when you're surrounded by mountains." He pointed down the road. "Take a left at the next intersection, then follow the signs for about a mile. You can't miss it."

"Much appreciated," Hatch said.

The attendant turned and began walking back toward the station. Hatch climbed back into the car and pulled out of the lot.

Following the directions she'd been given, Hatch soon spotted a sign directing her to the Clifton Jail's visitor parking area. She pulled off the dirt road and scanned the surrounding desert landscape for a suitable spot to conceal her vehicle. Her eyes settled on a grouping of tall, imposing saguaro cacti a short distance from the lot.

Carefully navigating her car off the main road, Hatch felt the tires crunching against the rocky desert terrain. She cut the headlights and maneuvered the vehicle into the midst of the saguaro cluster. The cacti's thick, columnar shapes provided a natural barrier, breaking up the outline of her car and making it less conspicuous from a distance.

Satisfied with her chosen parking spot, Hatch turned off the engine and stepped out into the arid desert air. She took a moment to acclimate to her new surroundings, standing behind the green-hued pleated trunk of the largest saguaro. Spines jutted outward, fiercely guarding the cactus's vibrant pink fruit. Hatch reached into the gear bag in her trunk and retrieved two spare magazines, sliding them into the cargo pockets on the left side of her khakis. She then adjusted the position of her Glock, moving it from the small of her back to her right hip for easier access.

With her equipment in place and her vehicle concealed, Hatch set off towards the Clifton Jail, her senses heightened and her mind focused on the task at hand.

EIGHTEEN

Chapter 18

AMY LINDEN SAT IN THE DAMP, DIMLY LIT CELL, THE DRIPPING WATER from the stone ceiling above marking the passing seconds as each droplet fell into the growing puddle below. The disorienting effect of the chloroform was compounded by the timelessness of the rocky prison. She turned her attention to the young woman sharing this horrid experience.

Jenny, who had been in the underground confinement for over two weeks, seemed lost, tucked into the shadow-soaked corner with her arms wrapped tightly around her legs. She rocked ever so slightly, her vacant eyes like bottomless caverns.

From the little Jenny had spoken, Amy gathered that the torture she'd endured had not yet resulted in direct physical abuse. Regardless, the psychological damage was catastrophic.

Amy's mind raced with thoughts of escape. Her husband's words echoed in her mind: everyone thinks they know how they'll react when things go bad, but most find out how wrong they were. He'd been referring to the field training of rookie cops, but the principle applied here. Amy's experience as an ER nurse had exposed her to traumas that others, like Jenny, were not privy to. Having hardened herself to such situations, she now harnessed that resilience to strengthen her resolve.

The significant cooling of the air indicated that night had fallen. Escape consumed Amy's thoughts, and somehow, she felt that time was running out. They had to act now.

Edging closer to Jenny, Amy noticed a metal water tray beside the young girl—the same tray she had been forced to drink from since her captivity began. Jenny's dull eyes looked through Amy, her cheeks hollow from malnourishment. Amy's heart ached for her, but she knew pity wouldn't secure their freedom. She paused, a plan forming in her mind.

The kidnapper with the bandaged arm had walked outside, and Amy caught the acrid scent of cigarette smoke wafting in. Her eyes darted to the cell door. They were alone, but for how long?

Placing a hand on Jenny's shoulder, Amy felt the younger woman jerk back. "It's okay. It's me." She waited until a glimmer of recognition flickered in Jenny's sunken eyes. "I have a plan. I think I can get us out of here."

Jenny began shaking her head, slowly at first, then faster as she pressed herself against the rock wall. "No. We can't. They'll hurt us."

"I won't let that happen." Amy wasn't sure if she was convincing herself or her cellmate. "We can do this, but I need your help."

Jenny's eyes widened, tears forming as her voice crackled. "I don't think I can. I'm too... scared."

"Me too. But together, we're stronger." Amy picked up the dog dish and dumped out the remaining water before placing it in Jenny's hand. "This is your weapon now."

Jenny studied the stainless-steel bowl carefully. When she looked back up, the embers of defiance had been stoked. "What's your plan?"

Amy scooted closer, Miguel's valiant attempt to save her life at the forefront of her mind. She wouldn't allow his bravery to be in vain. His act had given her an opportunity, and she was determined to seize it.

HATCH PULLED OUT HER CELLPHONE, inserted one earbud into her left ear, and called Banyan. He answered on the first ring.

"I'm in Clifton."

Banyan's garbled response was indecipherable. Hatch hoped he could at least hear her. Recalling the gas station attendant's words, spotty at best was an understatement. "Comms are going to be bad. Signal is garbage. I'll keep this call open." As the last bit of sun disappeared behind the western mountains, Hatch added, "I'm moving in on foot."

Emerging from the cactus cluster, Hatch paused to get her bearings. The jail lay below, accessible by a winding staircase from the lot. Glancing back at her concealed car, she was satisfied it would remain unnoticed during her reconnaissance. Hatch set her sights on the rocky outcropping north of the jail, a natural vantage point that would provide an ideal spot to observe the entrance and monitor any activity.

The hill continued to rise until she reached the overlook, approximately one hundred yards from the jail. The relatively flat, open space was scattered with large boulders, offering potential cover and concealment if needed. Hatch lay flat against the ground and low-crawled to the edge.

From this vantage point, she had a clear line of sight to the jail's south-facing main entrance and the small courtyard in front. A dark-colored SUV and a heavily tinted panel van were parked nearby. Two men stood guard, the glowing embers of their cigarettes piercing the darkness as they smoked in silence, their postures relaxed but alert.

One of the guards, his left forearm wrapped in a bloodstained dressing, stubbed out his cigarette and headed inside. His partner seemed unconcerned about being left alone, continuing to puff on his cigarette.

Opportunities were rare and needed to be seized when presented. With only one guard remaining, the odds had tipped in Hatch's favor, and she had no intention of letting this window close.

NINETEEN

Chapter 19

LINDEN'S HEART RACED AS HE PULLED THE RANGE ROVER INTO THE parking lot of the Jumping Cholla motel. His mind consumed with an incurable worry for his wife's safety and the dread of facing his children empty-handed. He was sure Carver kept the details to himself, just giving enough to convey the seriousness without inducing panic. Linden had raised his children to attune to their surroundings, to trust their instincts.

The journey from the Rusty Spur had been a blur. He'd spent the whole drive rehearsing and replaying what he'd tell his children. Each time, the words fell short. He circled back to the nagging truth that his choices had caused a chain of events that now jeopardized the chance they'd ever see their mother again. He'd been the outsider looking in on too many tragedies to count over his twenty-plus years of service as a police officer. None of it had prepared him for how to handle it now that the tables were turned.

Bringing the SUV to a stop, he let it idle for a moment before cutting the engine. Linden's firearms training from his days on the force came to mind, reminding him of the importance of remaining calm and focused in high-pressure situations. As the setting sun glared through the windshield, he closed his eyes and took a deep breath, counting to four. He held it for four, released it for four, and held it again. Linden repeated this breathing exercise for another minute or so, until he felt his pulse slow and a modicum of calm return. The familiar routine helped ground him, steadying his nerves before facing his children with the grim news.

He opened his eyes again to see that Banyan sat unmoved in the passenger seat. "Just needed to get a grip."

"No better way than a little combat breathing." Banyan held no judgement in his eyes as he spoke. "Why don't you take a few minutes to settle in with your kids. I'll check in with the motel owner and make sure everything's kosher with the add-on to our guest list."

Linden nodded. "Thanks. For everything."

Banyan nodded and opened his door. A rush of warm air filled the vehicle's interior. "No need to thank us. We haven't done anything yet."

Linden stepped out. Banyan walked away toward the main office. Linden lingered for a moment outside of the room's door. He could hear the television and the muffled murmur of his children's voices responding to the antics of the cartoon characters.

He knocked gently. The children quieted. Linden saw the slightest movement at the curtain before he heard the rattle of the chain latch followed by the metallic thud of the deadbolt's release. The door opened and Carver greeted him with a nod.

The smell of pizza filled his nostrils. Mia and Ethan abandoned their slices and rushed to him. Linden dropped to one knee to receive them, taking one in each arm and pulling them tight. He never wanted to let go. Emotion overwhelmed him. He fought to choke back its release.

"Daddy, I knew you'd be okay." Mia's whispered voice didn't hide her worry.

He gave her a kiss on the cheek. It was his son's words that rocked him back to the reality of the circumstances. "Where's mom?"

Linden separated himself enough to look Ethan in his eyes. His mouth opened, but no words came out. He looked away, blinking rapidly as his throat tightened.

"Why don't we let your dad get settled in?" Carver put a hand on Ethan's shoulder, the soft whirring of the air conditioner unit filling the brief silence. "Better eat your pizza before I do." He mussed the boy's hair.

Ethan snagged a slice on his way back to the bed. Mia joined him. For once, Linden was glad for the distraction their mindless television shows provided.

Standing, he spoke in a low whisper. "Thanks." He shook his head. "Not sure I would've been able to give him an answer."

Carver stepped toward the open door to close it. "Any word?"

"Nothing. Still waiting to hear from Banyan's partner." Linden sighed heavily. "You trust these people? Think they can really do something to help?"

"They come highly recommended from a man who I'd trust with my life. So, yes. If they're able to help, I'd trust them implicitly."

"We're in the eye of the hurricane right now. What we do next to find her matters. Every second counts." Linden looked back at his children with a mix of emotions clouding his expression."

BANYAN STEPPED INTO THE OFFICE, his eyes drawn to the stuffed snake with the missing rattle. It seemed to be eyeing him back as he approached the counter. Before he could tap the brass bell, Ernie emerged from the back office.

"How's your daughter doing?" Banyan asked.

Ernie's expression softened. "Much better. She's resting now, but the antivenom worked its magic. The doctor says she'll be up and running in no time."

The fatigue was evident on the motel owner's face, but the panicked worry from earlier that morning had dissipated. "Glad to hear," Banyan said with a nod.

Ernie glanced past him. "Where's your friend? I wanted to thank her properly."

"She's doing a little sightseeing but will be back later. I'll be sure to pass along your gratitude."

"Please do. I'm forever in her debt."

"Did you get the note we left about our visitors?"

Ernie nodded. He opened the drawer under the desk and pulled out the cash they'd left. "Please take this. I can't accept. You've already done more than I can ever repay you for."

Banyan gave a dismissive wave. "I wouldn't think of it."

"Then what can I do to make your stay more comfortable?"

"Would it be possible to add another room? Our friends will need to stay the night."

"Of course." Ernie rummaged through the drawer. He set a key on the counter. "Next door to your room."

"Perfect, thanks." Banyan reached into his wallet.

"This time I must insist." Ernie was now the one waving a dismissive hand. "It's on the house. And there's no names in the book. Your friends are safe here with me."

Banyan put his wallet away. Giving Ernie an appreciative nod, he headed back out. The sun was closing in on the horizon. Long shadows stretched out across the desert landscape. He saw Linden standing with Carver outside the room's open door. Banyan tossed the key to Linden. "Got an extra room. Figured the kids might be more comfortable."

Banyan's phone buzzed, ripping his gaze away from the darkening scene outside the window. It was Hatch. He held up a finger to the other men who looked over at him as he put the cellphone to his ear.

"I can't hear you. Hold on." Banyan grabbed his earbuds and stuck them in his ears. He waited for a split second for the Bluetooth handoff. The noise cancelling did little to clear the line. Hatch's voice came through in staccato chunks, a mishmash of vowels and consonants. "You're still coming in choppy."

Banyan held his phone's screen out in front of him. He had a full signal. The interference must be on her end. A final burst of static came through. The only words he could accurately decipher were, "moving in." The call remained open, but communication had ceased.

Leaving the phone call active and the earbuds in his ears, he turned off the noise cancelling function as he stepped back toward the two men. Linden was visibly anxious.

"Sounds like she's on location."

"Any sign of Amy?" Lines of desperation creased his brow.

"Comms are bad." Banyan could see this wasn't the answer Linden was hoping for. "I'm keeping the line open. We'll know soon enough."

"In the meantime?"

"We start working on Plan B." Banyan tapped the strap of his backpack where he kept his laptop. "The kids seem pretty settled in there. Why don't we step into the other room and prepare our backup option." He paused for a moment before adding, "and hope we don't have to use it."

TWENTY

Chapter 20

AMY'S PLAN WAS IN MOTION, A DANGEROUS GAMBIT THAT COULD EITHER lead to their freedom or seal their fate. Calling out to the guard, her voice steady and calm, masked the thunder of her heart. "I'm a nurse," she said, her words echoing off the dank walls. "I can patch up your arm properly."

The guard eyed her, his grip tightening on the rifle slung across his chest. "It's just a scratch," he said, his heavily accented English tinged with disdain. "No need to fuss."

Amy persisted, her voice taking on a more urgent tone. "If that wound isn't properly cleaned and dressed, you risk developing a serious infection. Cellulitis, sepsis, even necrotizing fasciitis—trust me, you don't want to take that chance." Holding his gaze, her eyes conveyed the gravity of her words. "I've seen it happen before, in the ER. It's not pretty."

He scoffed. "You worried about me? You should be worried about yourself."

By the looks of him, he had likely endured worse injuries. She needed to convince him otherwise. "Maybe I should explain. That last one I mentioned, necrotizing fasciitis, it's a rare but deadly bacterial infection that can start from the smallest of cuts. The bacteria gets into your body through a break in the skin and start multiplying rapidly. They release toxins that destroy the tissue around the infection site."

His eyes moved from Amy's to the bandage on his arm. "What happens then?"

"The infection spreads quickly, causing severe pain, swelling, and fever. If it's not treated immediately with antibiotics and surgery, it can lead to sepsis, organ failure, and even death. In some cases, they might even have to amputate the affected limb."

He grunted, then looked back up at her. "You're full of shit."

He was calling her bluff. Amy kept her poker face. "Suit yourself. Not my arm. But you should know the location of your cut is a prime spot for the bacteria to enter your body. Be sure to thank whoever did that bandage because it looks like it hasn't been properly cleaned." The guard hesitated, his resolve wavering. Amy could see the seed she'd planted was taking root. "I really think you should let me take a closer look at it and maybe clean it out for you."

"Why would you care?"

"Consider it a trade." Her voice lowered. Amy was using the same persuasive tone she'd used to win arguments with her children. "I patch your arm, and you give us some proper food. Something other than scraps." She looked over her shoulder. "She's not doing well. She needs nourishment."

The guard's gaze flickered to the dark corner where Jenny sat, then back to Amy. A slow, predatory smile spread across his face, sending a chill down Amy's spine. Afraid the desperation she felt would seep into her words, she held her tongue and pressed no further.

He looked down the dark corridor before reaching for the cell door with his uninjured arm. "Any funny business, and I'll make sure you regret it."

Rusty hinges protested. The guard stepped inside, leaving the cell door open behind him. Amy's heart raced. She willed herself to remain calm as she gestured for the guard to sit on the rickety cot nearby.

Amy edged closer to the wounded guard. He recoiled and looked as though he was going to lash out at her. The moment passed, and he extended his bandaged arm in her direction. She feigned a gentleness that belied her intentions. She unwrapped the dressing, revealing the ugly inflamed wound beneath. It was a deep laceration. She nearly smiled as she sent a silent prayer of thanks to Miguel.

Amy's mind flashed back to her days in the ER, to the countless wounds she had treated over the years. She prodded around the swollen skin. "Does this hurt?"

He muttered something through gritted teeth in his native tongue.

Good, she thought, *then this is going to feel like a flaming poker.* Amy plunged her thumbs into the open wound, twisting and gouging with all her strength.

The guard let out a howl of agony, his body convulsing in pain. He reared back just as Jenny lunged from the shadows. Two weeks of pent-up anger came out in one savage explosion of violence as she slammed the metal dish against the side of the guard's head with a sickening thud. The guard crumpled to the ground, his rifle clattering to the floor.

Amy wasted no time. She tugged on the leather strap, but the rifle was pinned beneath the unconscious man's thick torso. She reached for the pistol on his hip and pulled it free from his holster. Her hands trembled as she sought to remember the instructions her husband had given her during their few visits to the shooting range. "Run!" she shouted to Jenny, her voice raw with adrenaline and fear.

The two women sprinted for the open cell door. Amy slammed it shut behind them. A groan rumbled forth from the guard who was now on all fours. He looked more beast than man, a werewolf in mid-transformation. His pain roared out, echoing off the stone walls.

Jenny stood frozen, staring down the corridor. Amy grabbed her by the shoulder and gave her a firm tug. "It's now or never." Amy pressed the gun out in front of her and led the way. Jenny followed close behind, still clutching the metal tray like a shield.

As they ran through the twisting cavern of the jail, the guard's voice rose behind them, shouting in Russian. The harsh, guttural words bounced off the cave walls, a haunting soundtrack to their desperate escape.

United in their bid for freedom, the women charged forward.

HATCH SPOKE IN A WHISPER. "Banyan, do you copy?" She listened to the responding crackle of static in her earbud. "I count two. Parties are separated. Target of opportunity." No response. She was on her own. The tactical decisions defaulted to the operator on the ground. Hesitation had been her enemy once before. Never again.

Hatch crept along the rocky path outside the Clifton Jail, her footsteps careful and measured. The darkness enveloped her, the moonlight casting eerie shadows across the jagged terrain. Moving with purpose, her senses heightened, acutely aware of the delicate balance between speed and stealth.

With one inside the jail, it left a solitary guard standing watch. It was an unfair advantage, Hatch mused, but one she would gladly exploit. The guard seemed relaxed, casually smoking a cigarette under the dim glow of a single light bulb. The illumination would work in Hatch's favor, blinding the guard's night vision and making it difficult for him to spot her movements in the shadows.

She had about twenty feet of rocky path to descend before reaching level ground. Hatch's muscles tensed as she navigated the treacherous footing, her eyes scanning the surroundings for any signs of danger. The silence was broken by a loud metallic clang from within the jail—the sound of a cell slamming shut.

In the eerie quiet that followed, a male voice reverberated from the depths of the building. Though the words were in Russian, the angry tone left little need for translation. Hatch quickened her pace, sensing the momentary advantage was running out.

Hatch was still darting along the uneven trail when two women burst from the dark tunnel entrance. Leading the charge was Amy Linden. The second was a younger woman. Hatch guessed by the tattered clothes and gaunt features that this was the girlfriend of Linden's informant who had disappeared in the weeks prior.

The guard standing by the entrance dropped his cigarette. He staggered back, putting distance between the charging escapees while reaching for the AK-47 slung over his shoulder. Amy was faster, her pistol was pointed out in front of her and aimed steadily at the man's chest.

"Don't move, or I'll shoot!" Amy's voice rang out, filled with a mixture of fear and determination.

The guard froze. The assault rifle was free from his shoulder and held along his side. Hatch watched the man inching his hand toward the trigger housing. He raised his left hand up in a half-hearted attempt to surrender.

"Drop the gun!" Amy's voice cracked under the stress.

The guard didn't lower the weapon. He remained still. His eyes locked on the woman holding him at gunpoint.

Hatch slipped her pistol from its holster and kept it tight against her ribcage. Her eyes focused on the gunman ahead. The van would provide her cover once she broke free from the rocky path.

A noise came from inside the jail. Amy's head turned ever so slightly. But it was all the gunman needed. In the split-second of distraction, Amy had lost sight of her target. She was now facing down the Kalashnikov's long barrel.

"You drop it," the gunman snarled.

There was a moment's hesitation. Amy let out a whimper as the defiance evaporated into the warm Arizona night air. Slowly, she bent down, lowering the pistol to the dirt beside her feet.

All was not lost. The other guard had yet to emerge from the jail. The gunman was still alone, and thoroughly distracted.

Hatch took the final steps to ground level when her foot caught on something hidden in the darkness. She tried to right herself, but whatever had tripped her snagged the top of her boot. She braced for the fall.

Just before hitting the dirt, Hatch heard the clang of metal against a nearby rock. It sounded like a can. Hatch's training kicked in, a split second of recognition before the realization hit her. Tripwire. Grenade.

She dove forward from the outcropping, her body twisting in

midair and turning away as the device detonated. A blinding flash and deafening bang filled the air, the concussive force of the flashbang disorienting her senses.

Hatch scrambled across the rocky ground, vision flickering with spots of light. She pawed at the dirt, but a heavy boot pinned her gun hand to the ground. Looking up, she struggled to focus on the looming silhouette of a large man, the barrel of his rifle aimed at her face. A smile played across his shadowed features.

As his face came into focus, a sinking feeling settled in her gut. In her desperate attempt to save the two women, she'd failed to notice the third guard providing overwatch. Anger and self-recrimination coursed through her veins, she was trapped and mentally berating herself for the oversight.

The short-term effects of the flashbang began to subside. The ringing in her ears faded, and Banyan's faint, intermittent voice crackled through her earpiece. "Hatch? I heard the blast. Are you okay? Hatch, can you hear me?"

Before she could respond, the butt of the rifle swung down with brutal force. A sharp pain exploded in her head, and darkness enveloped her.

TWENTY-ONE

Chapter 21

BANYAN SAT IN THE MOTEL ROOM WITH LINDEN AND CARVER, HIS MIND focused on the mission at hand. The last transmission from Hatch came through, and the sound of an explosion—a flashbang—filled the room. Banyan's heart raced as he began preparing to go, knowing every second counted.

He turned to Linden, his voice steady but urgent. "Linden, you need to stay here at the motel and keep watch over your children. Carver and I will go to Hatch's last known location, the Clifton Jail. It's about two and a half hours from here."

Just as Banyan was about to head out the door, Linden's phone rang. The color drained from his face as he looked at the caller ID. It was from a private number. His hand trembled as he answered the call, putting it on speaker so Banyan could listen in. His voice was tight with barely contained anger. "Where's my wife?"

"You have big balls. I'll give you that." Egor's laughter crackled through the phone. "You've made a grave mistake." His accented voice dripped with venom. "By involving outsiders, you've only made things worse for yourself... and your pretty wife."

While Linden responded, Banyan ushered him over to his computer and plugged the phone into his laptop. He had to act fast to track Novik's location. He quickly launched a specialized software program designed to triangulate the origin of the call using cell tower data.

"Keep him talking." Banyan mouthed the words. His fingers danced over the keyboard. "The longer he stays on the line, the better chance we have of pinpointing his location."

Carver leaned in, looking over Banyan's shoulder at the screen. "What exactly are you doing?"

"I'm using a technique called multilateration," Banyan said, his eyes never leaving the screen. "Basically, I'm measuring the time difference between when the signal reaches different cell towers. By comparing these times, I can calculate the phone's position relative to the towers and narrow down its location."

Linden's grip tightened on the phone, his knuckles turning white. "What do you want?"

"What I've been asking for all along," Egor replied, his tone almost casual. "You will secure the release of my brother within twenty-four hours."

"I can't get his parole approved that fast."

"No. Not approval. I want him released."

"Impossible," Linden said. "I don't know what power you think I have, but I can't just snap my fingers and get—"

"Don't tell me what you can and can't do. You are not the white knight you claim to be. And you will find a way to get him out, just like you found a way to put him in."

Linden was visibly flustered. Banyan gave him a roll of his finger, encouraging him to keep him talking.

"I need more time."

"Twenty-four hours. And the clock is already ticking." Egor's laughter turned cold. "Maybe you need more motivation. How about every hour you're late, I send you a piece of your beloved wife?"

"You sick bastard! I'll—"

"You'll do nothing except release my brother from prison. Is that clear?"

"Please. Don't...don't hurt her. I'll do it. I'll find a way."

"It's amazing how long someone can live, even as they're being taken apart piece by piece."

The blood drained from Linden's face. Egor hung up, leaving Linden with nothing but the sound of his own ragged breathing. He turned to Banyan. His eyes were wide with desperation. "Did you get a lock on the call?"

"These guys know what they're doing." Banyan shook his head, his face grim. "The call was routed through multiple servers, bouncing all over the place. Impossible to trace."

Linden sank onto the bed, his head in his hands. "I can't do it. There's no way I can get Anton released."

Banyan closed his laptop and stood up. He placed a reassuring hand on the man's shoulder. "You might not be able to. But I can."

HATCH'S CONSCIOUSNESS came in flashes. Snapshots of light, captured for the briefest of moments before fading away. Her skin tingled against the cool, damp floor. Muffled voices ebbed and flowed. She tried to push herself upright and was greeted by a throbbing pain in her head, a stark reminder of the rifle butt that had struck her.

It took another minute or so before her senses began to sharpen. That's when Hatch became acutely aware of a presence leaning over her. Coiling back, ready to strike, a sudden realization hit her—the person kneeling beside her was female. Hatch blinked her eyes until the woman's features came into focus. It was Amy Linden, whom Hatch recognized from the recent photo Linden had shown her of his wife and two children.

Hatch studied Amy's face, etched with concern. The woman's lips moved, but Hatch couldn't make out the words over the persistent ringing in her ears. She gave a slight nod, hoping to convey that she was alright, as her faculties slowly returned.

Amy used a torn piece of her own shirt as a makeshift rag and gently tended to the wound on Hatch's forehead. The cool fabric provided a small measure of relief against the searing pain.

"You've got a pretty bad gash. I've been able to stop most of the bleeding." Amy set the rag aside and re-examined the injury. "Good news is there's no fracture. Or at least, none that I can see."

"I've been told I'm a bit hardheaded." Hatch made a weak attempt at a smile. She fought through the discomfort and brought herself to her knees. "Thanks for patching me up."

"You'll probably need some stitches. But I've done what I could here."

Hatch took in her surroundings. She wondered what the former tour guide turned gas station attendant would think of the renovations. They were trapped inside one of the jail's cramped, musty cells. The bars cast long shadows across the floor.

"I guess introductions are in order. I'm Amy."

"Yes, I know."

"Did my husband send you?"

"Not exactly." This was a situation where truth held more value than deception. But in Hatch's world, truth was a luxury she rarely could afford. She opted for the less is more approach. "Max Carver asked us to look into some threats your husband had been receiving."

"Guess they proved to be valid." Amy glanced at the scar on Hatch's arm. "You said *us*. Does that mean someone else is out there? Is there a rescue planned?" Amy spoke in a hushed whisper.

"Why would it matter? The last one turned out to be a huge success." The voice crept out of the shadows nearby. There was a bite to her words.

"That's Jenny," Amy said. "She's been here a while. Optimism isn't at a high right now."

"Understandable." Hatch turned her attention to the sheepish woman tucked into the darkest corner of the cell. "Your boyfriend is working with Amy's husband to get you out."

Hatch's mention of Jenny's boyfriend caused the timid woman to stir, but not enough to leave the safety of her dark shroud.

Amy seemed to have a better outlook and faced their current circumstance with an air of confidence. Right now, that made Hatch her best ally. Jenny was suffering from the effects of the long-term confinement. She would be an x-factor or none at all.

Hatch scooted away from the cell door, putting as much distance as possible between herself and the guards. Not one to sit around and wait for a rescue party, she needed to assess the situation and begin looking for a way out of this nightmare.

"We still don't know your name?" Amy asked.

Hatch thought about using an alias, or even the codename Tracy had come up with for her. Neither option felt right. Human beings under extreme stress needed a sense of connection. Establishing trust early could pay huge dividends later. "People usually just call me Hatch."

"Hatch it is then." Amy's eyes made a second pass over the scarred arm. "You've handled situations like this before?"

"Each is different. But the short answer is yes."

"So what do we do, just wait for the cavalry?"

"We wait for an opportunity."

"We already tried that and failed." Jenny shook her head, the defeat evident in her eyes. "You did too."

"You tried. And you managed to get the best of one of the guards." Hatch paused until Jenny met her gaze. "Proves you're both fighters. That's not failure in my book."

A flicker of something—hope, perhaps—danced in Jenny's eyes. Hatch pressed on, her voice growing stronger. "Besides, the only way I'm out of the fight is when I'm dead and gone. And last I checked, I'm still breathing."

The faintest hint of a smile tugged at the corners of Jenny's mouth. It was a small victory, but Hatch would take it.

Hatch focused on the muscular man with a thick black beard and bald head, the same man who'd gotten the drop on her. They all had tattoos like the one Linden had described–the snake with a woman's head, identifying them as property of the Novik family. But this man had another tattoo that stretched along the left side of his neck. It was a black bat descending from a parachute and holding a knife–a mark Hatch recognized from her time working private security contracts in Afghanistan. It signified the man was a former member of Russia's elite Spetsnaz special forces.

His military background explained the sophisticated booby trap that had caught Hatch off guard. It also made clear she was not dealing with a run-of-the-mill group of thugs. These were highly trained professionals, and the fact that an ex-Spetsnaz operator was now working for a Belarusian mob group was not surprising–skilled mercenaries often took lucrative private contracts with criminal organizations after leaving military service. Hatch silently vowed not to underestimate them again.

A phone vibrated on the table and the man with the bandaged arm answered. The conversation was one-sided. The guard only responded once, acknowledging he understood, before the call ended. He said something to the other men. All three shifted their gaze to the women trapped behind the bars, but remained seated at the table, engrossed in discussion.

Seizing the opportunity while the guards were distracted, Hatch leaned in close to Amy and the other captive woman. "Do what they say until I say otherwise," she whispered, their hushed tones inaudible to the guards across the room.

Amy scooted closer. "Where'd you learn all this?" she asked in a low voice.

A weak smile played across Hatch's lips. "At the corner of everywhere and nowhere."

Hatch's head continued its relentless throbbing, the pain a constant reminder of the guard's brutal assault. The private conversation was cut short as the guards abruptly rose from the table and approached the cell, the man who had knocked Hatch out leading the way, his eyes gleaming with malice. He moved his gaze along each of the female prisoners.

"Time for a little ride, ladies. Turn around and walk backwards to the bars. Nice and slow."

Hatch exchanged a glance with Amy and Jenny, their faces etched with fear and uncertainty. They had no choice but to comply. Hatch moved first, leading the way towards the bars.

The bearded guard let out a derisive laugh and turned to the one with the bandaged arm. "Try not to let these women get the best of you again."

Hatch watched a flicker of satisfaction roll across both women's faces. Small victories won big battles.

"Turn away. Clasp your fingers together and reach your wrists through the bars," the guard ordered.

Hatch, Amy, and Jenny did as they were told. The guard produced a handful of zip ties and secured their wrists, the plastic biting into their skin.

"Lean your heads back."

The hard iron of the bar sent a ripple of pain through her skull. A hand gripped her around the throat and pulled her tight. Hatch braced as a gag was forced into her mouth and tied off. She tasted something sickly sweet assaulting her senses. She tried to hold her breath, slow the effects, but a moment later her world was plunged into darkness as a burlap sack was tugged over her head, the rough fabric scratching against her face as it was cinched tight around her throat.

The guard's rough handling repeatedly slammed Hatch's head into the bars with a dizzying effect. She bit back a cry of pain, determined not to give him any satisfaction.

Released from the guard's grip, Hatch staggered forward, her balance thrown off by the disorienting darkness of the sack. She could hear Amy and Jenny's muffled breaths beside her, their movements just as unsteady.

The sweet taste on the gag grew stronger, and Hatch realized with a sinking feeling that it was laced with chloroform. The drug began to take effect, her limbs growing heavy and her mind clouding.

Desperate to maintain some semblance of control, Hatch took a knee, lowering herself and hoping to minimize the impact of the inevitable fall. She tried to warn Amy and Jenny, to urge them to do the same, but her words came out as garbled grunts, lost in the folds of the gag.

One by one, they collapsed, their bodies hitting the hard, unforgiving floor of the cell. Hatch fought against the pull of unconsciousness, her lungs burning as she tried to slow her breathing. But it was a losing battle.

The cell door creaked open, the sound distant and muffled to

Hatch's fading senses. Heavy footsteps approached, the vibrations echoing through the stone beneath her cheek. Clinging to the last shreds of awareness, her mind raced with desperate plans and fading hopes.

But the darkness was relentless, and as the chloroform's grip tightened, Hatch felt herself slipping away. The footsteps grew closer, the guard's shadow a black abyss that swallowed her whole.

TWENTY-TWO

Chapter 22

THE MORNING SUN PEEKED THROUGH THE MOTEL ROOM CURTAINS, casting a warm glow on Linden's face. He glanced over at his children. Mia and Ethan were still sound asleep. The worry for their mother's safety had kept them up late into the night, until exhaustion finally took hold.

Linden hadn't slept except for the occasional nod of his head. He kept watch throughout the night. His vigilance to protect his children and fevered concern for his wife were enough to keep him awake for the foreseeable future.

Stepping outside, the sunlight slapped him in the face. Linden's stomach knotted. He was reminded of the many all-nighters he'd pulled as a cop and how he never got used to the effects of watching the next day's dawn without sleeping off the preceding one.

Tapping the outside of his pant pockets, he searched for a pack of smokes. He wanted nothing more than the burning sensation of a cigarette to stave off the edginess. He'd officially quit years back, when Ethan was born, but he'd kept a secret stash and dug one out from time to time. He was pretty sure Amy knew, but she'd never said anything.

The motel owner was sweeping the walkway clear of the desert sand blown across the lot during the night. He looked over at Linden and gave a friendly wave. He set his broom against the wall and walked over. "How was your stay?"

"Just fine." Linden struggled to make small talk.

"Doesn't look like you slept much."

Linden took notice of the man's features, the dark circles under his tanned skin. "I could say the same about you."

The motel owner nodded. "My daughter was bitten by a rattler yesterday morning."

The worry lines made sense now. "Is she okay?"

"Yes. Much better now. If it hadn't been for your friend—the woman with the scar on her arm—it would've been a different story."

Linden listened intently, as the motel owner recounted how Hatch had found his daughter, carried her over a mile, and saved her life. Banyan had been right when he'd said his partner was as tough as they come.

"She's my world, you know? I wouldn't know what to do without her." His voice tinged with emotion. "My wife died in a car accident a few years back. It's been devastating for my daughter. She hasn't spoken since."

Linden felt a pang of empathy. The thought of losing his own wife and the impact it would have on his children was almost too much to bear. He needed to change the subject, to clear his mind. "Hey, you wouldn't happen to have a cigarette, would you?"

"I don't smoke. Not anymore."

Linden nodded. "Me neither."

The motel owner cocked an eye. Both men chuckled. It felt good and loosened some of the unrelenting worry pressing down on him.

Tires crunched, causing Linden's gaze to shift to the roadway. Involuntarily his hand moved to his hipline where his Glock was holstered inside his waistband, concealed by his untucked shirt. His body relaxed when he recognized the vehicle. Banyan and Carver had returned from Clifton.

Banyan had called earlier to notify him there was no sign of his wife or the others. Linden knew his wife was still missing but seeing them return from their mission empty-handed made the truth all the more real.

"I best let you get on with your day." The motel owner cleared his throat. "It's none of my business, but if I can be of any help, please don't hesitate to ask. Us fathers gotta stick together." He gave a friendly nod and returned to his broom.

Banyan parked the car and walked over to Linden. "Any word from Egor?"

Linden shook his head.

"Looks like we're going forward with Plan B, then," Banyan said.

"Do you think it'll work?" Linden was doubtful he'd managed to mask the desperation in his voice.

"It has to work. Failure is not an option, not in my world." Banyan's gaze hardened. "And I don't intend to start accepting it now."

HATCH'S EYES fluttered open and her mind climbed up from the depths of her chloroform-induced blackout. Fluorescent light from a rectangular fixture in the ceiling above penetrated through the fibrous crosshatching of a burlap sack covering her face.

The cool mustiness of the cavern jail was replaced by the warmth and brightness of the room. As her senses slowly returned, she began utilizing them to scope out her new surroundings. A distinct odor overtook the lingering scent of the chloroform, a scent that Hatch recognized immediately. The air was thick with the scent of jet fuel. Somewhere in the distance, the sound of a small prop plane could be heard taking off.

With a grunt of effort, Hatch manipulated her jaw until she freed the gag from her mouth. She licked at her dry lips, tasting the chemical residue. Hatch strained to listen for any signs her captors were present. Hearing none, she wasted no time.

She folded her body, bringing her knees up to her chest and tucking into a fetal position. Hatch worked her hands, still bound at the wrists, under her feet. The zip tie caught on the heel of her hiking boot, forcing the sharp plastic edge deeper into her flesh. She felt the blood coat her fingers as she continued to wriggle her arms until they were in front of her.

Hatch made quick work of ripping off the hood covering her head. The room itself was a small windowless office space.

She squirmed over to the nearest person. Amy was slumped on the floor and appeared to be unconscious. Shaking her shoulder, Hatch whispered urgently, "Amy, wake up."

A soft groan escaped Amy's lips in response, a sign that she was starting to come around.

Hatch removed the hood. She then loosened the knot and removed the gag from her mouth, leaving it to hang around her neck like a kerchief. Amy's head hung low, gently bobbing from side to side.

While Amy regained her senses, Hatch moved along the floor to Jenny and performed the same steps. It took several precious minutes, but both women gradually began to rouse from their chemical slumber. Their eyes blinked open, the disorienting effects of the chloroform leaving them foggy and confused.

"Where are we?" Amy slurred her words.

"Looks like we're at an airport." Hatch kept her voice low and signaled for the other two to do the same. "I heard a prop plane taking off. My guess is that this is a small airfield. Less eyes and different security protocols."

"How long have we been out?" Amy asked.

"Not sure." There was no clock on the wall and Hatch had been stripped of all her belongings, including her watch. "And I'm not sure how long we have until our friends come back."

"What's the plan?"

"Still working on it. Getting these flex cuffs off would be a good start." Hatch stood. The floor seemed to shift under her feet, causing her to wobble. She used a nearby desk as a crutch.

"Careful," Amy said. "The chloroform will leave you woozy."

Hatch nodded, taking a deep, cleansing breath to steady herself as she regained her balance. Her eyes scanned the space, searching for anything that could be used as a weapon or to free their restraints. But the drawers were locked, and she knew better than to expect their captors to be careless enough to leave such aids within reach. These men were trained professionals, as Hatch had learned the hard way. Unlike the movies, there was little to no chance they'd be lax enough to leave exploitable tools or objects accessible, especially after Amy and Jenny had previously gotten the better of them once before.

Papers were strewn across the desktop. Hatch's gaze swept over them until a particular document made her pause. It appeared to be a flight plan. Her eyes scanned the details, and a glimmer of hope sparked within her–the Noviks were planning a trip to Mexico, departing from Chandler Airport.

"Ever heard of Chandler?" she asked, turning to Amy.

The other woman nodded. "It's about halfway between Clifton and Phoenix."

Hatch felt a wave of relief wash over her. While still captive, they remained relatively close, which meant Banyan had a better chance of tracking them down. She knew he would be out there searching, and this new information could prove invaluable in narrowing his search radius.

Hatch's thoughts scattered as the unmistakable cadence of approaching footsteps echoed down the corridor. Time was up. In a final frantic sweep of the desktop, her gaze landed on a paperclip peeking out from beneath a sheaf of documents. With deft fingers, she swiped it and slipped it into her mouth, concealing the slim metal instrument between her teeth and cheek.

Moving quickly, Hatch crouched beside each of the other captive women, carefully sliding their black hoods back into place while leaving their gags hanging loosely around their necks. "Stay calm, but keep your wits sharp," she murmured under her breath. "When the chance arises, any action is better than inaction."

The heavy footfalls drew nearer with each passing second. Hatch positioned herself on the floor alongside Amy and Jenny, her body tense but her expression impassive as the cell door clanged open.

Hatch barely managed to pull the hood over her head and get her wrists behind her back before the door clanged open. Darkness enveloped her, the coarse fabric scratching against her skin as she blinked rapidly, struggling to adjust to the sudden absence of light.

"Time to wake up." The low, gravelly voice sent a chill down her spine–the man who'd assaulted her. "It'll all be over soon."

There was a chilling finality in his tone, but Hatch refused to let fear take hold. Her jaw clenched, and she subtly flexed her bound wrists, the paperclip's sharp edge biting into her flesh as a silent reminder of her determination. By the day's end, she vowed, this man would eat his words.

TWENTY-THREE

Chapter 23

LINDEN LOOKED ON AS BANYAN SAT HUNCHED OVER HIS LAPTOP. THE past several hours had been fueled by a combination of caffeine and adrenaline. Banyan was relentless in his efforts to backdoor his way into the Arizona Department of Corrections database. The soft glow of the screen illuminated his face.

Carver returned with three cups of steaming coffee balanced precariously in his arms. "Somebody order room service?"

Linden was bleary-eyed. The long night had stretched into a longer day, and he wasn't sure another cup could jumpstart his motor. "How are the kids doing?"

"They're good as can be. Made friends with the little girl who lives here."

Linden had been engrossed in his desperate attempt to meet the demands. Although he could do nothing more than stand by and watch, he felt compelled to do so. Warm steam bathed his face as he sipped at his cup. He resumed his post and looked on, a mixture of desperation and hope etched into his features.

Without breaking stride, Banyan lifted his cup with one hand while continuing to type with his other. "Alright, I'm almost through. Just need to bypass the last firewall and then we should be in the system."

"I feel like you've been saying that for the last four hours." Linden was unable to hide the frustration in his voice.

"Not as easy as it looks. For what I'm attempting to do, and considering the level of security I'm up against, four hours is pretty damn good." Banyan rubbed his eyes. "The Arizona State Correctional system has a pretty robust network, with multiple layers of protection. I had to start by running a series of port scans to find a vulnerability I could exploit."

"You're speaking a foreign language to me."

"Think of it like checking all the doors and windows of a house to see if any are unlocked. In this case, I was checking all the potential entry points of the network to find a weakness. Once I found one, I used a SQL injection attack to gain initial access."

"This is why I don't ask." Carver leaned in, giving Linden a nudge.

"It's a technique where I insert malicious code into a website or application to manipulate the database behind it. In this case, it allowed me to bypass the authentication and get a foothold in the system. From there, I've been working my way through the network, escalating my privileges and cracking encryption keys as I go." Banyan continued to talk, more to himself as if he was running through a mental checklist. "Well, I also had to be careful not to trigger any alarms. I'm using a VPN and spoofing my IP address to hide my location, and I've had to pivot through multiple servers to make my traffic harder to trace. It's a delicate dance, but I'm almost there... and... I'm in!"

Linden nearly dropped his cup. "You've got access?"

"Full admin rights. Now I just need to find the inmate database and modify the release records. Give me a few more minutes and our guy will be walking out the front gate in a matter of hours."

To Linden's untrained eye, it was a jumble of numbers and letters, but to Banyan, it was a roadmap leading straight to their target.

"Okay, I've got Novik's file," Banyan announced, his voice tinged with excitement. He cracked his knuckles, a small smile playing at the corners of his mouth. "All I need to do is alter the parole decision and authorize his immediate release."

Linden leaned in closer, his brow furrowed. "How exactly are you going to do that without leaving a trace?"

"It's all about the timestamps. I'm going to make it look like the parole was approved in your original submission and that the authorizing authority scheduled the release for the following afternoon, which is actually today." A few keystrokes launched more lines of code. "Think of it like a digital magic trick. I'm manipulating the data, changing things to create a false trail. To anyone looking at the records, it will appear as though the decision was made through the proper channels, at the right time."

Linden nodded. "And the release time?"

"4 PM. We need to buy ourselves as much time as we can. If we can delay Novik's actual release until the afternoon, it gives us a window to try to locate your wife before the exchange."

"And if we don't?" Linden knew the answer but asked anyway.

"Then we make the exchange. Carver and I will do our part to make sure it goes smoothly."

Banyan leaned back in his chair, a triumphant smile on his face. "It's done. Anton Novik's parole has been approved, and his release is set."

Linden let out a breath he hadn't realized he'd been holding, a flicker of hope igniting in his chest. "Thank you."

With the pieces in motion, a new sense of urgency filled the room. Linden went to the bathroom to freshen up before making the trip to Florence.

TWENTY-FOUR

Chapter 24

HATCH MADE NO EFFORT TO MOVE. SHE REMAINED MOTIONLESS WHEN she first woke on the floor of the small office somewhere in Chandler Airport. Best for them to assume she and the others were still unconscious. No need to put them on alert. These men were well-trained, and she hoped her ruse was effective enough that they wouldn't notice the fact her gag was no longer covering her mouth.

Through the veiled lens of the hood, she watched as boots approached. Meaty hands gripped her without warning. In one swift movement, Hatch was jerked upright and tossed against the desk behind her.

Her back was pressed against one of the desk's legs. Sour breath penetrated the fabric separating her from the man in front of her. His dark eyes held a savagery to them as they hovered inches from her face. The manhandling did little to improve the pulsing throb radiating from her injured forehead. Through it all, Hatch remained limp.

Hatch could sense the two women next to her being handled in the same rough manner by the other men present. Unlike Hatch, they were unable to contain the whimpers of pain.

"Let Egor know they're up from their beauty sleep," the one monitoring Hatch said as he stood.

The kidnapper furthest from Hatch left the room. When the door opened again, she heard two men enter. Fingers snapped, and in a blur of movement, the hood was ripped from her head. She saw the man standing over her had given an extra second's attention to the status of her gag. Before he could address it, the former Spetsnaz soldier was interrupted.

"I hope you've found our hospitality to be to your liking." Egor Novik stepped deeper into the small room. A devious smile crept across his face as his gaze swept over the women, pausing briefly to evaluate each captive.

Egor stepped closer. He now stood only a few feet from Amy. "You look terrified. Not to worry. If your husband does as he's instructed, then all will be over soon." He leaned down, gripping her underneath the chin, he forced her to meet his eyes. "Do you think he'll do that? Or is he going to test my conviction?"

A flash of anger rippled across Amy's clenched jaw. She pulled her chin free from the man's hand. "Guess we'll have to see."

"You've got some fight in you, I see. I like that in a woman." Egor straightened. "I'd have to cut that out of you."

Amy's eyes spoke to the disgust she felt, but she swallowed down any words to back it. Hatch was glad to see she hadn't let emotions get the best of her. This was not the time to test the limits of their captor's patience. The advantage was not in their favor. Not yet, at least.

"He's not so good at following the rules. He proved that when he arrested my brother." Egor's attention turned to Hatch. "And he did it again by sending an uninvited guest to the party. What is that saying... three strikes and you're out? Looks like he's down to one more chance."

Hatch cocked her head, just enough to send a look of defiance but not so much that he'd fear she would be capable of delivering on her unspoken promise. He didn't step closer. He treated her with a degree of caution he didn't offer the other two women.

"I see Volk has given you a new scar to add to your impressive collection." Egor gave a nod of approval to the large man who'd gifted Hatch with her latest injury. "You're lucky to be alive."

"Luck is just opportunity by another name."

"Then it looks like you'll have an opportunity to see how that works out for you." Egor's eyes rested on the twisted branches of the scar extending up her arm. "Interesting. You know I heard stories from some friends of mine. Stories about a woman who went to Juarez. A woman who killed many members of the Fuentes Cartel. A woman with a nasty scar on her right arm."

Hatch felt an uneasiness settle over her. The past had a way of haunting people. But her past was far different from most. Her skeletons could fill ten closets. And from the sounds of it, Egor Novik had managed to open one.

"When we're done with all this business with my brother, my family and I are planning on taking a trip south of the border." Egor's tone was playful. "I think I'll have you join us. The cartels have a long memory and short temper. I wonder what kind of price you might fetch. If nothing else, offering you up will serve as a good faith gesture while we lay low for a while."

"They've tried to kill me before—yet here I am." Hatch's mood darkened, her eyes narrowing with defiance. "You may find out I'm more trouble than I'm worth."

Volk grunted. "I don't think so. You don't look so tough from where I stand."

"We'll have plenty of time to discuss this during our flight. Right now, we must deal with the problem at hand." Egor looked at his watch and then at Amy. "It's time to find out if your husband has done as he was told. If not, it'll get quite messy in here."

Egor stepped toward the door. Before exiting, he turned back. The rumble of a plane's engine reverberated along the corrugated metal walls of the room. "Feel free to scream all you like. No one will hear you." With a final unsettling smile, he turned and took his leave.

Hatch watched as the other men followed. Before leaving, Volk patted the top of her head. He tapped a long fixed-blade tactical knife on his belt. "You and I will spend some quality time together soon.

Maybe I'll give you a matching scar on your other arm. Something to remember me by."

"You'll regret not just killing me when you had the chance."

Volk shoved her head into the edge of the desk. Glittering stars filled her vision. She wrestled the pain into submission, giving him no satisfaction in what he'd just inflicted.

The impact had nearly caused her to swallow the paperclip tucked along the inside of her cheek. Using her tongue, Hatch worked the small but crucial tool back into place.

Volk kicked Jenny's legs out of his way before following the other men out into the hangar. The door closed. Aside from the noise of the plane, silence fell upon them. It was Amy who broke it.

"Who are you?" Amy whispered. "What did he mean about Juarez?"

"It's a long story. Let's just say that I've got some experience in dealing with people like the Noviks."

Jenny squirmed to move a little closer. "And you lived to tell."

"Sometimes the deciding factor when facing unbeatable odds is the will to win." Hatch recognized Amy's strength. She wanted to make sure Jenny found hers. "Willpower can move mountains."

"Aren't you afraid?" Jenny asked.

"Fear is a good thing. It's nature's survival serum. It heightens the body's senses and gives you a fighting chance. Anyone who tells you they're not afraid is lying. The truest measure of resolve is to recognize your fear and conquer it."

Hatch looked over at the door. She manipulated the paperclip along her cheek to the edge of her mouth. She spit it onto the floor alongside her thigh.

Amy eyed the saliva-covered fastener. "What're you planning on doing with that?"

"I'm going to get these cuffs off." Hatch shifted her body, twisting until she felt the moist metal. She gripped the paperclip tightly between her fingers and began unbending it, straightening it out into a thin, stiff wire.

She twisted her hands, the plastic cutting deeper into her skin. Hatch maneuvered the paperclip upward and into the locking mechanism of the zip tie, the small square part that prevents the tie from loosening once tightened. She blindly probed with the tip of the extended paperclip until she felt it insert into the tiny opening where the binding's ribbed surface passes through.

Hatch pushed the paperclip in deeper, wiggling it, feeling for the release catch inside the lock. After a few tense seconds of manipulation, she felt the paperclip lever the catch open slightly. The tie loosened a fraction of an inch around her wrists.

She continued working the paperclip against the catch again and again. The tedious process of releasing the catch was made more difficult by the trickle of blood moistening her grip. Hatch still hadn't managed to get the tie completely off, but after a minute of work, she had created enough slack to slip her hands out of the right-side cuff.

The other two women stared at her wide-eyed when she brought her hands around to her front. Hatch took a second to roll her wrists. The tingle radiating throughout her fingers signaled the much-improved circulation.

"Move over MacGyver," Amy said.

"Let's not pop the cork on the champaign just yet." Hatch used her makeshift key to begin the process of releasing the cuff on her left hand. The procedure was made easier now that she could see what she was doing and could use her right hand to do it.

"Where'd you learn to do that?" Jenny asked, impressed.

"Army."

Before she could explain her euphemism, the door to the room swung open. Hatch quickly returned her hands to the small of her back and slid her right hand into the loosened cuff. She resumed the effort of blindly working to release her left wrist.

Hatch watched as the thrill of hope she'd seen in Amy and Jenny was dashed as Novik's goon squad returned.

"It's time." Volk stood at the open door as the other two men entered.

The men hoisted both women from the floor and dragged them from the room. Amy shot a worried glance at Hatch before being led out into the hangar bay.

The door closed, leaving Volk alone with Hatch. The barrel-chested former special forces operator took a few steps closer. "Don't give me a reason to mess up that pretty face any more than I already have."

TWENTY-FIVE

Chapter 25

LINDEN'S HEART RACED AS HE SPED DOWN THE INTERSTATE TOWARDS Florence. The air was on full blast but sweat continued to bleed out from his pores. His eyes darted back and forth between the clock and the road ahead. Precious minutes ticked off, his mind calculating and recalculating the distance he had left on the drive to the prison. He should make it with ten minutes to spare. Linden had no interest in testing Egor's resolve. The Noviks had proven their word was binding, their threats were as good as a promise.

Momentarily transfixed by the clock, when he looked up, Linden saw the bright red of the cars stopped in all lanes. He cursed aloud as he slammed the brakes.

The Range Rover fishtailed before coming to a screeching stop mere inches from the rear bumper of a Subaru station wagon. His heart was already in overdrive and the near miss accident almost caused a cardio event.

There was no movement. He saw Banyan and Carver come to a stop three cars behind. The radio crackled with news of a three-car pile-up on I-10. The pitchy voice of the disc jockey only added to Linden's aggravation. "Anyone heading into Florence better call your wife and tell her you won't be home for dinner. Traffic is backing up in all directions. Looks like you'll be there a while." Linden cursed again, this time directing his slurs at the man feeding him this grave news, before turning it off.

He sat in silence. Two minutes had vanished. The last grains of sand would fill the bottom of the hourglass long before he got to the penitentiary. Hearing sirens, he watched as an ambulance blazed along its shoulder. It zipped by and the wailing faded around the bend as it headed on to the crash.

Linden turned the wheel, edging out into the breakdown lane. He followed the same path the ambulance had. Instead of sirens, Linden gunned it forward under the glares of the angry motorists he raced past, more than one offering him a one-finger salute. In his rearview mirror, he caught a glimpse of Banyan and Carver struggling to keep up after a box truck cut out in front of them.

The exit was less than a mile ahead. He made up for lost time once off the highway. Linden arrived at the prison with just minutes to spare. He parked in the same visitor lot he had the day before. This time, he made his way to the door right off the main entrance marked for prisoner release. There was a fence with razor wire lining the top that sectioned off a twenty-foot corridor from the prison exit to the locked gate where Linden now stood. The ex-cons Linden had the pleasure of dealing with over the years had described that last walk the longest of their lives.

Linden stood on his toes. He saw the man he'd spent the latter part of his career trying to put behind bars, receiving his exit paperwork. Anton Novik no longer wore the bright orange jumpsuit. He'd traded it for the clothes he was arrested in, a blue velour tracksuit.

He looked at his watch. It was a few seconds past the 4 o'clock hour. He looked back to the parking lot. No sign of Banyan and Carver. He returned his attention to the prison and saw Anton being led out by a corrections officer. Linden was thankful it wasn't the same one from the other day. It'd be hard to explain why the man he'd denied parole to was now being released into his care.

Linden's phone rang. He answered immediately.

"Put my brother on the phone," Egor growled.

"He's coming out now." Linden's heart was in his throat.

"Playing games will cost you." He paused long enough for a woman's voice to squeal in the background. "Which part of your wife would you like to receive first?"

"No games. Promise. I can see him now. Just give me a–"

"Perhaps I will start with ears." Egor cut him off with a voice cold enough to make ice jealous. "Easy to remove. And the bleeding is bad but manageable. Or perhaps the eyes. Since you enjoy playing games, you can call the coin toss. Heads for ears, tails for eyes. What'll it be?"

At that moment, Anton stood on the opposite side of the gate. Linden pressed the phone against the chain links. "Tell him you're out."

"Brother," Anton said. "You've done good."

Linden retracted the phone. The guard gave him an inquisitive look, but Linden dismissed it and turned away. He spoke in a hushed tone. "Where are we doing this?"

"My brother will give you directions. I'd hate for you to run off and tell anymore of your friends." Egor rolled the 's' like the hiss of a snake. "It'll all be over soon. That is, if you do exactly as I say. You know what happens if you don't."

His heart leaped as he heard his wife's voice on the phone, a heartfelt "I love you" that told him she was still alive. Then the call ended. The gate behind him closed. Linden turned to face his nemesis as the guard retreated inside the prison.

"Together again." Novik's lip curled upward. "You chose to do things the hard way. I like that. More fun for me."

Leading Anton to the Range Rover, he opened the passenger side. As he closed the door and walked around the back of the SUV, he scanned the lot. There was still no sign of Banyan and Carver. Sinking back into the warm leather of the driver's seat, he wondered if he was alone.

Linden drove in silence. He slowed as he neared the exit of the prison's parking lot. "Head to SR-79 North."

"Where are we going?"

"Chandler Airport. I have a plane to catch."

Linden did as he'd done throughout his career when facing a potential crisis. He played out the scenario over and over again in his mind until he found a solution. This time he found none. He hoped over the next forty-five miles he'd come up with one.

TWENTY-SIX

Chapter 26

OUTSIDE THE HANGAR BAY, THE PROP PLANE IDLED IN PREPARATION FOR takeoff. The low, steady hum of the engine permeated the air. The constant background noise continued to reverberate within the confines of the small office space, serving as a reminder of the next destination Novik had in store for Hatch if she didn't find her way out.

Volk rested himself against the desk opposite Hatch. He seemed uninterested in her, only shooting the occasional side-eyed glance in her direction. His pistol was tucked in a drop-down holster secured to the outside of his right thigh. The knife he'd threatened her with was in a worn leather sheath above.

She slid her wrists out of the cuff loops but kept her hands behind her back. Hatch shifted her weight and slid her feet close. Coiled like a snake, she slowly moved her hands forward into a ready position. She clutched one loop of the flex cuff in her left hand and balanced herself with the right.

Hatch launched from her crouched position, launching herself into the air and causing the man in front of her to jump. With the deftness of an Olympic hurdler, she vaulted over the desk and towards Volk. Papers were flung to the floor as she zipped across the metallic tabletop toward her intended target.

For a big man, Volk moved quickly. But not quick enough. Hatch, with her lightning reflexes, closed the gap before he could fully spin to face the advancing threat. His hand darted towards the pistol at his side, desperate to defend himself.

Hatch, anticipating his move, slammed her body into his with all her might while lashing the zip tie around his neck in one swift motion. She yanked back with a fierce determination, the loops cinching down on both of her hands. Volk writhed and pinched his lips as the plastic dug into the skin around his throat, constricting his airway.

Refusing to surrender, Volk thrashed violently, his hand gripping the pistol as he frantically worked to release it from the holster. Hatch, aware of the imminent danger, swiftly pinned his arm to his waist, wrapping her right leg around him in a vice-like grip. She locked it in place by hooking her ankle behind her left knee, forming an unbreakable triangle with her body that glued her to Volk's back, rendering him immobile.

His left hand remained free, and he alternated between elbow strikes and punches over his shoulders, desperate to break free from Hatch's relentless grip. Hatch dipped and weaved her head, narrowly avoiding the punches he lobbed. But there was no avoiding the devastating impact of his elbow as it crashed into her gut with a sickening thud. She exhaled hard, the air forcibly expelled from her lungs, but she tightened her core, determined to maintain her hold. Through it all, Hatch managed to keep her chokehold, the plastic biting deep into her fingers, leaving angry red marks on her skin.

Volk's movements gradually slowed, his struggles becoming more labored with each passing second. It was only a matter of time before the restricted blood flow deprived his brain of enough oxygen to render him unconscious. Hatch squeezed her legs tight, applying pressure to his diaphragm, hoping to expedite the process and bring an end to this grueling battle.

He staggered forward, his massive frame swaying, and bent at the waist. It looked as though the giant was about to fall, succumbing to the effects of the chokehold. Without warning, Volk mustered his remaining strength and threw himself back, a last-ditch effort to dislodge his attacker.

Hatch, still clinging to his back, was now airborne. She couldn't do anything but hold on for the ride, her hands clutched to the zip tie, and her legs locked above his waist in an unyielding grip. There was no way to deflect the coming impact, and she braced herself for the inevitable collision with the floor.

The impact was brutal. Hatch's back slammed into the smooth surface of the concrete floor with a sickening thud. The air was forced from her lungs as she found herself sandwiched between the massive former Spetsnaz soldier and the solid, unyielding flooring. Despite the jarring collision, Hatch had managed to tuck her chin to her chest before landing, minimizing the damage to her head and enabling her to retain consciousness.

Volk, seizing the opportunity, wasted no time in trying to capitalize on his last-ditch effort to turn the tide. The collision with the floor had separated Hatch's legs, and she no longer maintained control of his right arm. With a quick motion, he thumbed the retention button, releasing the pistol from the holster.

Desperation fueled Hatch's actions. She stomped the heel of her boot down on the big man's hand, slowing the draw. Thinking on her feet, she threaded her left foot inside his thigh and twisted her body while scooting out from under him. Hatch continued to hold the zip tie as tightly as she could, but she knew she no longer had the leverage.

She tried to lock him with her legs, but he fended off her attempt with a grunt. Undeterred, Hatch managed to sweep him, causing him to topple to his left side. The shift enabled her to shimmy out from under him, her heart pounding in her chest.

In a matter of seconds, the gun would be in play. She couldn't allow it to happen. Failure was not an option.

With a burst of adrenaline, Hatch tugged her right hand free of the cuff. Volk choked out a cough, but before he could recover, her hand was already at his waist. She felt the handle of the knife, its presence a glimmer of hope in the chaos.

As the gun began its deadly motion, Hatch sunk the knife into Volk's back with a determined thrust. She plunged the blade upward between his ribs, just below the shoulder blade, feeling it slice through flesh and muscle. Volk's body stiffened as the knife found its mark.

Volk tried to cry out, but with his lung deflated, only a gurgling, raspy wheeze escaped his lips. No words, just a desperate, futile attempt at communication as he collapsed, his life slipping away. Hatch, her senses heightened, kicked the gun free from his hand. He made a feeble attempt to retrieve it, clawing at the floor with weakening fingers.

Without hesitation, Hatch mounted his back, her weight pressing down on him. She held the blade firm, feeling the warmth of his blood seeping onto her hand as Volk's resistance waned. Less than a minute later, the fight drained from him, pooling in a maroon puddle that spread out across the gray floor like a macabre painting. Hatch waited an additional thirty seconds, her heart pounding in her ears, before sliding her left hand along his neck. Finding no pulse, she released her hold and pushed herself back, the adrenaline still coursing through her veins.

Killing was always personal, but the intimacy of the knife made it even more so. Hatch looked down at her right hand, coated in the evidence of her actions. She wiped off what she could on the dead man's pant leg before standing up, her legs shaking slightly from the exertion.

As she stood there, catching her breath, Hatch's mind raced. The weight of the kill settled on her shoulders, but she knew there was no time to dwell on it. She allowed herself a few deep breaths, focusing on the rise and fall of her chest, before stepping over Volk's lifeless body and bending down to pick up his gun.

Standing by the closed door, Hatch was blind to the threat that lurked beyond. But she knew she had to face it. She cleared her mind, pushing aside the doubts and the guilt, and prepared herself to confront whatever lay ahead. With one more steadying breath, she readied herself to face the unknown head-on.

TWENTY-SEVEN

Chapter 27

THE SUN HUNG LOW ON THE HORIZON, PAINTING THE SKY IN VIBRANT hues of orange and pink as Linden steered his Range Rover into the Chandler Aviation complex. He followed Anton's terse directions, pulling the vehicle around to a hangar at the far end of the tarmac.

As they approached, Linden noticed the hangar bay doors were wide open. The nose of a Cessna aircraft protruded halfway out. The propeller spun lazily. The low hum of the idling engine filled the air. There was a solitary pilot inside. He was busy with his pre-flight checks and appeared not to notice them as they drove past.

Linden maneuvered the Range Rover to the far side of the hangar, parking just outside the corrugated metal wall. He kept his gun aimed at Anton.

"Stay put," Linden ordered, his voice low and stern. "Don't even think about trying anything."

Linden exited the vehicle, keeping the gun leveled at his captive through the window. He circled around to the passenger side and yanked open the door.

"Out. Slowly," Linden commanded.

Anton stepped out, his movements deliberate. As soon as both feet touched the asphalt, Linden jabbed the muzzle of the pistol into Anton's back. With his other hand, he grabbed a fistful of Anton's shirt at the nape of his neck and twisted it tight.

"Walk," Linden growled, propelling Anton forward.

Linden guided Anton along the side of the hangar, the warmth of the day's heat radiating off the corrugated metal. With the setting sun at their backs, he scanned the area continuously, alert for any signs of an ambush. About halfway down the hangar wall, a gray door came into view.

Linden tightened his grip on Anton's shirt and quickened their pace, eager to get inside and out of the open. With each step, Linden's mind raced, wondering what new danger awaited them on the other side of that door.

"When we get inside, remember that you may hold the leverage, but I'm still holding a gun."

"You do as you're told, and this will be over." Anton looked over his shoulder. "You don't and your wife will be dead. You will be dead. Then I'll head over to the Jumping Cholla motel where your children are staying. And they too will be dead."

Rage surged within him at the mention of his children. How did he know where they were?

Anton gave a knowing smile. "You left your key in the cupholder." He turned away as he continued to speak. "You're getting sloppy. Maybe retirement has dulled your edge. Prison only served to sharpen mine."

"Don't speak about my children again." Linden's finger danced on the trigger housing. He considered ending it right here and now.

"I won't have to. Just as long as you don't screw this up."

Linden exhaled, clearing his mind from horrific thoughts assaulting him. He focused on the here and now. "Open it." His voice steadied, his composure returning.

Anton offered no further ominous threats. He did as Linden instructed and opened the door to the hangar.

As Linden stepped into the hangar, he took a moment to adjust to the overwhelming smell of jet fuel that assaulted his nostrils. The constant hum of the plane's engine flooded the space, its vibrations reverberating off the metal walls, creating an eerie atmosphere. Across the expansive bay, a door to a small office creaked open, drawing his attention.

Egor Novik emerged first, his presence commanding and intimidating. Following closely behind him was a woman, who Linden assumed must've been Burner's girlfriend, Jenny. She was ushered to a metal folding chair, her movements tentative and uncertain. A short, brutish man took up guard behind her, his stance menacing and protective.

Linden's gaze swept the hangar, searching for a familiar face. His heart skipped a beat when he spotted Amy on the far side of the bay. At the sight of her, his knees buckled, threatening to give way beneath him. Despite the gravity of the situation, she held her head high, a testament to her inner strength. But even from a distance, Linden could discern the fear that lurked beneath her brave facade. Their eyes met, and a flood of memories washed over him.

He remembered the first time he'd laid eyes on her, the moment he realized that love at first sight wasn't just a cliché. For him, it had been an instantaneous and irrevocable connection. Amy, on the other hand, had taken some convincing. But after several months of persistent courtship and heartfelt gestures, she'd finally said yes. In that moment, as they stood amidst the chaos and danger, Linden made a silent vow to himself. This would not be their last encounter. It was up to him to ensure their future together.

Linden's attention was drawn back to the present as a man with a bandaged left arm roughly shoved Amy into another seat, positioning himself beside her like a sentry. Every instinct in Linden's body screamed at him to shoot the man for daring to touch his wife in such a manner. However, the sight of the thug's injured arm brought a flicker of satisfaction to the corner of Linden's mouth. If they managed to survive this nightmarish ordeal, he would have to give Miguel a well-deserved raise for his valiant efforts.

"Let's get this family reunion over with," Linden yelled across the room, hoping to be heard above the hum of the plane. "Send my wife to me and I'll release Anton."

"That is not how this will go. You do not call the shots." Egor looked over to the man on his left. Amy was yanked from her seat. "You will let my brother go. When I am satisfied, I will send your wife over."

Linden didn't trust a word he said but had no choice but to follow the orders. He tugged Anton back and whispered in his ear. "If my wife doesn't make it to me, I'll cut you down."

"You're not in a position to be making such claims," Anton snarled.

He shoved Anton forward and released his grip. The head of the Novik crime family staggered a step before taking up a confident stride towards Egor. Linden kept his gun trained at the center of the man's back. He squatted low, making himself a harder target.

Anton crossed over the halfway point. Amy hadn't moved. Linden swallowed the dread.

Egor turned to the man with the bandage. A simple nod of his head was all it took for his order to be carried out.

Amy sprinted past Anton. She looked back to Jenny who remained their captive. An unspoken apology was sent.

Linden absorbed his wife into a tight embrace when she reached him. Fearing the worst and knowing they were far from safe, he tucked her behind. He kept his gun pointing toward the Novik clan, loosely scanning each one with the sweep of his barrel while edging back toward the door he'd entered through.

"Almost there, baby. Just through that door." He spoke just loud enough to be heard above the whine of the engine.

"What about Jenny? We can't just leave her," Amy pleaded, her voice tinged with concern.

Linden met her gaze, his resolve unwavering. "We won't. I'll figure it out. I promise. But I can't do anything until I know you're safe."

As they neared the door, a flicker of movement caught Linden's eye. A shadow detached itself from behind a hulking aircraft tug parked along the wall. Burner emerged, his arm outstretched, a pistol aimed squarely at Linden's chest.

"Hold it right there," Burner commanded, his voice cracking with tension. His eyes were bloodshot, and a fresh bruise adorned his cheekbone. "Drop the gun, nice and slow."

Linden shifted his aim, locking eyes with his former informant. Desperation radiated from Burner's every pore. "What the hell are you doing?"

"Please!" Burner shot a frantic glance towards Jenny. The stocky man nearby now had his gun pressed against the back of her head. "I've got no choice."

Linden's mind raced, searching for a solution. "It doesn't have to end this way. Let's find a way, like we've done in the past." An idea formed, risky and daring. He knew if he deliberated too long, he'd lose his nerve. "Shoot me."

"What are you doing?" Amy hissed, disbelief coloring her tone.

"Trust me. It'll be okay." Linden kept his focus on Burner, his voice low and steady. "Center mass. Don't miss."

Burner faltered, his hand trembling. "I—what?"

"I'm wearing a vest. Take the damn shot. They want me dead. Take the shot. Get Jenny back, and then we'll deal with these assholes."

Egor's booming voice cut through the tension. "I'm tired of this little game. Shoot him, or I will kill your girlfriend."

Linden steeled himself, praying the vest would do its job and Burner's aim would be true. A gunshot rang out, the sound reverberating through the hangar.

Instinctively, Linden glanced down at his chest, expecting to feel the impact of the bullet against the vest. But realization dawned on him—the shot had come from the other side of the hangar. He whirled around, his eyes widening as he witnessed the scene unfolding before him. All hell had broken loose.

TWENTY-EIGHT

Chapter 28

HATCH STOOD POISED AT THE DOOR. SHE'D BEEN READY FOR THE OTHER members of the Novik crew to come barging through. The whine of the engine had provided enough of a noise cancelling barrier to mask the struggle of moments ago. Pressing herself closer, she heard another factor which likely contributed to the unnoticed killing of Volk. There was yelling. Something in the hostage negation was breaking down.

She turned the knob with her left hand. Volk's semi-automatic pistol firmly seated in the other, tinged with the dried blood of her enemy. Hatch flattened the gun against the center of her chest in a low-ready position.

She inched the door open, listening at first. Egor was barking a command. He was close, maybe only five or ten feet from the door. Hatch heard the response come from across the noisy bay. It was Linden. It took a second for her to decipher the conversation. Linden was directing his pleas to someone else.

Hatch opened it further. Linden was yelling at the man standing in the shadows, holding a gun as he shielded his wife behind him. He held a gun pointed out in the direction of the threat. As the shadowy figure stepped into the light, Hatch recognized him. It was Linden's informant, the man she'd seen him with at the bar.

The exchange had been made, Linden's wife for Anton Novik. Jenny was still held captive, apparently being used as leverage against Burner. She was seated in a metal folding chair. One of the kidnappers stood guard behind her, holding a gun to the back of her head. The one with the bandaged arm was a few feet away to his right. And just beyond stood Egor and Anton Novik, the crime family reunited. Attention was focused on the standoff unfolding before them. Anton had a look of amusement.

Hatch created an ad hoc plan of attack. Outnumbered and outgunned, she needed to capture the element of surprise.

Hatch stepped into the hangar, her left hand cupping the gun to strengthen her grip. She pressed it out in front of her, pausing briefly to align the front sight post with her intended target. Without hesitation, she fired two shots.

The guard holding Jenny hostage barely had time to react before the back of his head exploded into a red mist. Hatch felt the gun's recoil, but her focus remained unwavering as the man dropped to the ground.

Jenny's scream pierced the air, her body showered in the dead man's blood. Hatch swiftly shifted her aim to the next closest target— the thug with the bandaged arm. Before she could squeeze the trigger, a volley of return gunfire forced her to dive to the floor.

Bullets peppered the corrugated steel of the office's exterior wall, mere inches from where Hatch had been standing seconds before. She rolled once and fired several rounds of covering fire as she ran out of the hangar, seeking cover.

A second wave of gunfire dimpled the steel along the edge of the hangar bay door where Hatch crouched. The setting sun behind her cast an orange glow across the Cessna's fuselage to her left, as the pilot readied for takeoff.

Hatch waited, deaf to the approaching threat. Exposing herself without knowing the enemy's position would be a fatal mistake. In the game of death, action always trumped reaction, and she refused to be on the losing end of that equation.

A glimmer caught her eye. The Cessna's shiny exterior served as an improvised mirror, revealing the man with the bandaged arm cautiously closing the distance.

Hatch assumed a prone position, flattening herself against the warm tarmac. She cocked her right leg, keeping a watchful eye on her target. Two quick combat breaths cleared her mind, sharpening her focus.

With a powerful kick, Hatch propelled her body along the oil-stained ground. She twisted to her side as she broke from cover, extending her pistol. The man with the bandaged arm caught the movement, but it was too late. By the time he corrected his aim, Hatch had already fired three bullets, each one punching through the center of his chest. For good measure, she sent a fourth bullet straight through his forehead.

As the man with the bandaged arm crumpled to the floor, his body oozing red, Hatch surveyed the hangar for her next shot. Anton was nowhere to be seen. The standoff between Linden and Burner was now obscured by the Cessna's tail section.

Hatch's attention was drawn to Jenny, who staggered forward, her eyes wide with fear. For a moment, Hatch assumed shock had gotten the better of her. But then she noticed Egor's hand gripping Jenny's shoulder, using the traumatized young woman as a human shield.

Egor had been standing next to Jenny the entire time, but Hatch's focus on the immediate threats had caused her to overlook his presence. Now he shoved Jenny forward, only ten feet away from the steps leading up to the open door of the plane.

Realizing the gravity of the situation, Hatch retreated behind the wall. She needed to draw Egor out from behind his human cover if she had any chance of stopping him. To do that, she would have to put herself in the line of fire.

Taking a deep breath, Hatch stepped out from behind the hangar's exterior wall. She trained her gun at the void just above Jenny's shoulder, careful not to endanger the innocent woman. "No way you're getting on that plane!" Hatch yelled over the scream of the engine.

"You shoot, she dies," Egor threatened, his voice cold and calculated. He remained hidden behind Jenny, making it impossible for Hatch to get a clean shot.

Hatch side-stepped, desperately searching for an angle, but found none. Egor edged closer to the plane, now only a few feet away from the first step. The realization dawned on Hatch—Egor would never let Jenny go. She was his ticket to escape.

Hatch's mind raced, trying to formulate a plan. She knew she had to act fast, or Egor would slip away, taking Jenny with him. Every second counted as the plane's engine roared, ready for takeoff. Hatch steeled herself, preparing for the most crucial shot of her life. She had to find a way to neutralize Egor without harming Jenny, and she had to do it now.

Hatch stepped out from behind the wall, her shadow stretching across the tarmac, nearly reaching Egor and Jenny. She trained her gun on Egor, her voice steady and commanding. "Let her go, Egor. It's over."

Egor's grip tightened on Jenny's shoulder, his eyes narrowing. "You're in no position to make demands. One false move, and she dies."

Training and experience kicked in as Hatch ran every conceivable option. If she had any chance of taking the shot, she needed Jenny to move. Though not a common practice, shooting the hostage offered a remote possibility of taking the advantage. However, the domino effect had to be perfect. The shot location needed to be a target area that would produce the least possible likelihood of death while causing the hostage to move in such a way as to present a target of opportunity. All of this had to happen with such precision that the captor wouldn't have time to pull the trigger. Weighing the odds against the current circumstances, Hatch deemed this was not a viable option. The problem was, there weren't any others outside of a miracle.

Patience was her ally now, and the dire situation tested her resolve. In that moment of quiet desperation, Hatch noticed a change in Jenny's expression. The fear of moments ago was replaced by something else—angry determination. Their eyes met for a split second in an unspoken agreement.

"You don't have to do this, Egor," Hatch said, her voice softening. "Let Jenny go, and we can end this peacefully."

Egor sneered. "You think I'm foolish enough to believe that? No, she's my ticket out of here."

Just then, Jenny twisted away, catching Egor off guard. Bright sun seemed to temporarily blind him, and Hatch seized the opportunity. She squeezed the trigger, ready to take the shot.

But before she could release the round from her gun, Egor's head rocked back, a red arc extending from his forehead. He crumpled to the ground, his lifeless body falling away from Jenny.

Hatch turned to see where the shot had come from, shielding her eyes against the setting sun. In the distance, atop a storage building, she saw the glint of a scope and the silhouette huddled behind it. Banyan.

With all the targets neutralized except for Anton Novik, Hatch gave a two-fingered salute to her unseen ally before turning her attention back to the hangar. The standoff was over, but the mission wasn't complete. She had to find Anton and put an end to this once and for all.

TWENTY-NINE

Chapter 29

LINDEN WATCHED AS HATCH SINGLEHANDEDLY WAGED WAR WITH NOVIK and his crew. "Get out of here," he shouted to his wife.

Amy shook her head. "Not without you."

"No debate. I can't focus if I have to worry about keeping you safe." He jutted his chin toward the door, only a few feet from where they stood. "Car's running. I'm right behind you."

As Amy turned to leave, Linden's attention was drawn back to Burner, who still had his gun pointed in Linden's direction. In the chaos of the moment, Linden had nearly forgotten about the standoff with his former informant.

"Look!" Linden pointed toward the gun battle. "This is your chance to escape."

Tears welled up in Burner's eyes as he caught sight of his girlfriend, Jenny, now being used as a human shield by Egor Novik. "Jenny," he whispered, his voice breaking.

Linden saw the desperation in Burner's eyes. "I'll save her. Just put the gun down. I can't do it with you waving that thing around."

Across the hangar, a solitary gunshot put an end to Hatch's standoff with Egor. Jenny was safe. Suddenly, a shadow moved behind Burner, cutting in and out of the equipment lining the wall. A muzzle flash illuminated the dark space, and Anton emerged, clutching a pistol in his hand.

Burner screamed as Anton's bullet found its mark. In an involuntary reaction, Burner's finger tightened around the trigger, and a second shot rang out from his gun before he collapsed to the ground.

The round slammed into Linden's chest, striking him just below the sternum. The impact was like a sledgehammer blow, driving the air from his lungs and sending him staggering backward. His vision blurred as he struggled to draw breath, the pain radiating outward from the point of impact.

Linden's legs gave way, and he toppled backward, colliding with Amy. They crashed to the hard concrete floor in a tangle of limbs, Linden's weight pinning her beneath him. For a moment, he lay there, stunned and gasping, his ears ringing from the gunshot and the throbbing pain in his chest. Anton sprinted past him and disappeared through the door.

Amy's muffled cries pierced the haze of pain and confusion. With a groan, Linden rolled to the side, freeing her. Amy scrambled to her knees, her hands shaking as she tore open his shirt, desperate to assess the damage.

"The vest," Linden managed to gasp, his voice strained. "It caught the bullet."

Relief washed over Amy's face as she saw the bullet lodged in the Kevlar vest, mere inches from Linden's heart. She helped him sit up, supporting his weight as he struggled to catch his breath.

Across the hangar, Hatch's standoff with Egor continued, Jenny still held hostage. Linden knew he had to act fast to save her and put an end to this nightmare once and for all.

She fumbled with the Velcro straps of his vest, her fingers slick with sweat and trembling with adrenaline. Finally, she managed to undo the fastenings and push the soft Kevlar padding aside. Her hands roamed over his chest, searching for any sign of blood or injury.

As the realization dawned that the vest had done its job, Amy rocked back on her heels, choking back a sob of relief. Tears streamed down her face as she looked at Linden, the fear and worry in her eyes slowly giving way to gratitude and love.

Linden sat up and managed a weak smile, his voice hoarse as he spoke. "Told you I'd never leave home without it." A promise he'd made long ago, one he was glad he kept.

The calm in the storm had passed, disrupted by the wail coming from the man who'd shot him. Burner clutched his leg and writhed on the blood-soaked concrete. Amy rushed to his side. Over the noise of the plane's engine, Linden could hear his Range Rover speeding away, likely carrying Anton Novik inside.

The gunfire on the other side of the hangar had ceased. He looked over to see Egor and his men scattered across the bay, all of them painted in their own blood. Jenny was running toward Burner, tears streaking along her face.

Hatch wasn't far behind. She approached more cautiously, her head on a swivel, her body tense.

Linden stood, swaying still from having the wind knocked out of him, and holstered his weapon. He took a second to adjust his vest back in place. He plucked the small caliber round from the twisted hole. He slipped it into his pocket and planned to keep it as a souvenir, a talisman linking him to the day he dodged death. As Linden buttoned up his shirt, he reminded himself that this day was not over, and that Anton Novik was still out there somewhere.

HATCH BURST through the open door into the hangar bay, her senses on high alert. Behind her, a sudden change in the plane's noise caught her attention. The once steady hum of the idling engine had ceased, replaced by the eerie sound of the propeller blades slicing through the air as they continued to spin. The whooshing noise grew slower and quieter with each passing second, like a giant fan gradually winding down as the plane's propeller made its final rotations.

Within moments, the hangar was enveloped in complete silence, the absence of sound almost deafening. Hatch's footsteps echoed on the concrete as she cautiously approached the direction of the gunshots, her heart pounding in her chest.

The fleeting sun had made its final retreat, thrusting the bay's interior into a dim patchwork of shadows. Hatch's eyes scanned the area, taking in the scene before her. Jenny stood motionless, trapped in the mental prison of terrifying trauma, her eyes wide and unseeing. Hatch passed her, completing a rapid triage of the situation and focusing on the immediate threat at hand.

Up ahead in the din of the hangar, Hatch's gaze fell upon Amy, who was bent over on the floor. Hatch's heart caught in her throat, a surge of fear coursing through her veins. She raced toward her friend, her mind racing with the possibilities of what she might find.

As Hatch drew closer, the scene before her became clearer. It wasn't Amy who was injured, but Burner. He let out a cry of agony as Amy pressed firmly against the outside of his left thigh, her hands stained with his blood. Relief mixed with concern washed over Hatch as she realized that Amy was unharmed, but the situation was far from resolved. She quickened her pace, ready to assist in any way she could.

"Anton?"

"Son of bitch got away." Linden growled through grit teeth. "I can't believe I let—"

"Your wife's alive." Hatch redirected the retired cop's anger. "Won't be long before Anton's picked up. How far does he think he'll be able to get? Especially when we can track him."

"You're right."

Hatch and Linden made their way over to Amy. Jenny was now running toward her boyfriend, tears streaming down her face.

"How bad?" Hatch asked Amy.

Burner lay on the ground, groaning in pain, his left pant leg soaked with blood. Amy knelt beside him and continued applying pressure to the wound. "The bullet hit him in the outer thigh. It's likely missed the femoral artery, which is good news. If it had, he'd be bleeding out much faster. However, he's still losing blood, and we need to get him to a hospital as soon as possible."

A car screeched to a halt near the nose of the Cessna. Banyan hopped out and ran around to the trunk. He appeared a split-second later with a red duffle bag. He and Carver trotted toward them.

Banyan set the medical bag next to her. Amy glanced up at him. "I'm gonna need you to keep the pressure."

Burner flailed weakly, his skin starting to pale. Jenny dropped to her knees. She ran a soothing hand across his head. "Stay with me, baby. Please."

Amy's hands were soaked with blood, and she instructed Carver to open the medical bag and hand her the necessary supplies. Wiping her hands on her pants, she quickly put on a pair of latex gloves before grabbing a pack of sterile gauze.

"I'm going to pack the wound to help control the bleeding," she explained to Burner, keeping her voice calm and reassuring. "This will hurt, but it's necessary."

Burner nodded and then turned his glassy-eyed gaze back to Jenny. Amy set to work, carefully packing the gauze into the wound, applying steady pressure with the assistance of Banyan. Next, she secured a bandage tightly around his thigh, ensuring it was snug but not so much that it cut off circulation.

"That should help slow the bleeding until we can get him to a hospital," Amy said, sitting back on her heels. She checked Burner's pulse and nodded. "His pulse is still relatively strong."

"Ambulance is on its way." Carver slid his cellphone back into his pocket.

Hatch nodded as she looked around at the ragtag group assembled around the wounded man. "Carver, you stay with them." She shot a glance over at Banyan who was busy rinsing the blood from his hands with a saline solution. "Gonna need you batting cleanup when the cops arrive. Call Tracy and see what kind of interference he can run."

Banyan nodded. "Already done. I made the call when we were enroute. He's started working the angle on his end." He gave her a quizzical look. "And you?"

"I'm going after Anton." Hatch opened her phone. She tapped the icon for the GPS locator Carver had given them for Linden's Range Rover.

"Why don't we phone it in to the authorities? Let the boys in blue take it from here."

"I don't like the thought of someone else getting shot on our behalf." Hatch saw his unspoken agreement.

Linden huddled around Hatch as she examined the GPS tracking screen, their eyes fixed on the blinking dot representing the Range Rover. The dot moved steadily along the map, heading southeast from Chandler Airport.

"He's not taking I-10 towards Phoenix," Linden said, his brow furrowed in concentration. "It looks like he's sticking to the 87. He's already passed the exit for the 202."

"You sure?"

"If he were going to Phoenix, he would have taken that."

Hatch nodded. "So, if he's not going to Phoenix, where is he headed?"

Anton continued along Arizona State Route 87, passing through the town of Coolidge. The dot maintained its steady pace, showing no signs of slowing or turning.

"He's heading to Diamondback." Linden's voice was hollow. "The kids."

"He doesn't know where they are."

"He does." Linden cursed under his breath. "He saw the motel key in the cupholder."

"He's got a jump. Time to roll." Hatch put her hand out and caught the keys to Banyan's car in midair after he threw them. She started jogging out toward his vehicle.

"Wait!" Linden hurried after her. "No way I'm letting you go it alone."

"I work better that way."

Linden had a look of unfettered determination. "Those are my children."

Hatch wasted no more time debating. The two sprinted to the car.

"I should drive," Linden said.

Hatch didn't argue, tossing him the keys. She was in his world.

He'd be able to navigate the fastest possible route, leaving her to focus on tracking Anton's position.

An ambulance passed as they headed out of the gate. Linden gunned the car forward. They were minutes behind in a race where seconds counted. Hatch prepared her mind to stop Anton Novik from doing the unthinkable.

THIRTY

Chapter 30

HATCH SAT IN THE PASSENGER SEAT OF BANYAN'S CAR, HER MIND STILL reeling from the intense standoff at the airport. She rubbed at the dried blood clinging to her hands with a wet nap she'd found in the glove compartment, the coarse fabric scratching against her skin. Despite her efforts, Hatch knew from experience that no matter how hard she scrubbed or how clean she got, the invisible stain of the day's events would remain etched in her memory.

Beside her, Linden gripped the steering wheel tightly, his knuckles turning white as he picked off the miles, weaving in and out of traffic with expert precision. The car zipped along the highway, the engine humming as they raced against time. Since leaving the airport, Linden had been uncharacteristically quiet, his brow furrowed in concentration. Hatch gave the man space to sort through the stress of the standoff and the worry of the unknown challenges that lay ahead.

Glancing down at the GPS on her cell phone's screen, Hatch noted their progress. "We've made up some time," she said, breaking the silence. "We're only seven miles behind now, just a few minutes."

Linden's jaw clenched. "A lot can happen in a few minutes," he replied, his voice tight with tension.

Hatch studied his profile, taking in the determined set of his features. "Anton's really got it out for you," she observed, her tone a mix of concern and curiosity.

"I don't know where you'd get that idea," Linden retorted, cocking an eye in her direction, his words drenched in sarcasm.

"It's a rarity for a criminal to take things this far," Hatch continued, unfazed by his response. "Most would cut their losses and run."

Linden's grip on the steering wheel tightened. "You don't know Anton," he said, his voice low and serious.

Hatch leaned back in her seat, her gaze fixed on the road ahead. "But I know the type. Seen a lot of guys like him go down," she said, her words carrying the weight of experience. "Few retaliate. Fewer take it to this level."

Linden glanced at her, a flicker of interest in his eyes. "You were a cop?"

"Military Police," Hatch clarified, a hint of pride in her voice. "Worked in the Criminal Investigations Division before switching paths."

"And this makes you an authority on guys like Anton Novik?" Linden asked, his tone skeptical.

Hatch met his gaze, her expression serious. "It means I've seen my fair share of dangerous men," she said, her words carrying a warning. "And I know what they're capable of when pushed to the brink. From what I've observed, this situation seems deeply personal."

Linden's jaw clenched as he focused on the road ahead. After a moment of heavy silence, he spoke. "It is." He drove for the better part of a minute before continuing, his voice tight with emotion. "Anton was a slippery bastard. Like Teflon. Couldn't get anything to stick to him. Every case I tried to put on him fell apart."

"But you were eventually able to land one," Hatch said, her tone encouraging.

Linden shook his head. "Drugs and guns aren't the slam dunk they used to be. He'd be out in the next five years, tops."

"Which only adds to my assertion that his vengeance seems more personal in nature." Hatch's eyes flicked to a signpost, indicating they were two miles from Diamondback. "Trust me when I say this, I'm not one to judge. I'd just like to know what I'm getting into, seeing as how I'm about to go into battle for the third time in two days over it."

Linden let out a heavy sigh, the weight of his past bearing down on him. "I had Anton on a murder rap. Enough evidence to put him there. The difference this time was that I had a witness. A girl named Alyssa Park came forward and was willing to testify. I promised to protect her—to keep her safe." His voice faltered, the memory still raw. "But Anton was connected."

Hatch listened intently, watching as Linden's grip tightened around the steering wheel, his knuckles turning white. A painful expression swept across his face, the lines etched deep with grief and guilt.

"He found her," Linden said, his voice cracking. "Her body—what was left of her—was discovered a few days later."

"But you weren't able to pin it on him?" Hatch asked, her tone gentle.

"Like I said, Teflon." Linden's jaw clenched. "That's when I recruited the assistance of one of my informants."

"Burner," Hatch said, the pieces falling into place.

Linden nodded. "He'd helped me with plenty of cases in the past. For a junkie, he was extremely reliable. I ran a couple of busts, kept them off the books, and accumulated enough drugs and guns to make a strong case. Then I had Burner set up a deal with Anton." He glanced over at Hatch for the first time since they'd begun this conversation, his eyes filled with a mix of determination and regret. "And the rest is history."

Hatch met his gaze, her expression understanding. "From where I sit, you did the right thing. You played the hand you were dealt."

"Look where it's gotten me," Linden said, his voice heavy with the weight of his choices.

"You did what you needed to do," Hatch said, her tone firm. "Now we need to see this through."

Linden moved around a slower vehicle and took the exit, the car's engine revving as they approached their destination. "My kids—"

"Focus on the task at hand," Hatch interjected, her hand resting on Volk's pistol tucked under her thigh. "This ends tonight."

A couple minutes later, they passed the Copper Cactus Café. Hatch directed Linden to park Banyan's car just below the rise along the dirt road leading into the motel parking lot. They exited and quickly made the rest of the way on foot.

As Hatch and Linden approached the Jumping Cholla Motel, an eerie quietness enveloped them. The sun had set about an hour ago, and darkness had settled in, bringing with it a nocturnal symphony. A gentle chirping of crickets filled the warm air, occasionally interrupted by the distant hooting of an owl piercing through the cricket chorus.

A light breeze rustled the leaves of the cluster of trees at the edge of the parking lot. As they drew closer to the motel, the gentle hum of the building's exterior lights became noticeable, accompanied by the subtle electric buzz emanating from the intermittent flickering of the neon vacancy sign.

Linden's Range Rover was parked a short distance from the main office. The door to his motel room stood ajar, a foreboding sight that sent a chill down Hatch's spine.

Both Hatch and Linden drew their pistols, the metal cool against their palms. With a silent exchange of glances, they stepped from the cover of darkness and moved across the lot, sweeping wide to approach the room from different angles.

As they neared the backend of the Range Rover, they split off. Linden rounded the driver's side, while Hatch crept along the passenger side. She crouched low, reducing the crunch of her footsteps by moving heel-to-toe on the outside of her boot, minimizing any noise that might give away her presence.

At the front wheel well, Hatch paused. Heat poured out from the idling engine as she listened intently, her senses on high alert.

From within the room, Anton Novik's voice boomed, his tone menacing. "You say a word, and I'll come back for your little girl. Understood?"

A muffled response came from inside, the voice of a male speaking through what Hatch assumed was a gag, likely belonging to Ernie, the motel manager.

Then, a young voice spoke up, defiant despite the grave circumstances. "My dad will come. He'll kick your ass!" It was Ethan, Linden's son, his words filled with unwavering faith in his father's ability to save them.

Hatch's heart raced as she processed the situation. Anton had Linden's family, using them as leverage. She knew they had to act fast and with precision to ensure their safety. With a deep breath, she readied herself for the confrontation that lay ahead, determined to put an end to Anton's reign of terror once and for all.

Hatch heard the defiance in the boy's voice, recognizing it as the same bravery her nephew Jake demonstrated when he faced a similar situation at their family home in Hawk's Landing. Ethan was standing tall, serving as a protector for his little sister, even in the face of grave danger. Anton's response came swiftly in the form of a sharp slap.

The sound of the slap acted like a starter pistol, spurring Linden into action. He broke from cover and stepped forward, his gun extended, ready to take aim. However, he hesitated, not taking the shot.

Hatch had hoped to wait for an opportunity to catch Anton off guard, but Linden's move forced her into action. She stepped out, keeping low as she edged forward. Employing the tactical maneuver known as "slicing the pie," she slowly moved around the partially open door, gradually revealing more of the room's interior with each step.

As she positioned herself to get a clear view through the open doorway, Hatch quickly understood why Linden hadn't taken his shot. The scene before her eyes was a delicate and dangerous one.

Inside the motel room, Anton stood with his back to the door, his body shielding most of the room from view. However, the door was open wide enough for Hatch to see Ethan and his little sister huddled together on one of the beds, their faces etched with fear. Ernie, the motel manager, was bound and gagged on the floor nearby, his eyes wide with terror.

Anton held a gun in one hand, pointed in the direction of the children, while his other hand gripped Ethan's arm tightly. The slap had left a red mark on the boy's cheek, but his eyes still burned with defiance. He yanked the boy to the floor, tossing him like a ragdoll. His boot pinned the child to the floor as Anton scooped Mia from the bed and clutched her tight to him.

Mia's arms flailed. Her efforts only seemed to encourage Anton further. In one swift move, he transferred the firearm to its holster while drawing a long knife and holding it firm to the little girl's neck. This brought an end to her resistance.

Hatch knew that any sudden move could escalate the situation and put the children's lives at risk. She caught Linden's eye, silently communicating the need for a careful and calculated approach. They had to find a way to neutralize Anton without endangering the hostages, a task that would require all of their skill and cunning.

With her heart pounding in her chest, Hatch assessed the room, searching for any potential openings or vulnerabilities they could exploit. Every second counted, and she knew that the lives of Linden's family hung in the balance.

THIRTY-ONE

Chapter 31

ANTON'S FACE WAS A MASK OF CRUEL DETERMINATION, HIS EYES glinting with sadistic pleasure as he pressed the knife harder against Mia's throat. His foot was now pressing firmly on the unconscious boy's head. Ernie was tied to a chair, his mouth gagged. His daughter, Camila, clung to his side.

Mia whimpered, tears streaming down her face as she trembled in Anton's grasp. The metallic scent of blood mingled with the sweat and fear permeating the room.

Hatch's mind raced, calculating angles and trajectories, searching for any possible opening. She could feel Linden's desperation radiating off him in waves, his ragged breaths and trembling hands a testament to the impossible choice he faced.

Anton turned to the door, Mia tightly against his chest, her small body serving as a human shield. He positioned her head directly in front of his own, making it impossible for Hatch to get a clean shot without risking the young girl's life. The knife in his hand pressed against Mia's carotid artery, the blade gleaming menacingly in the dim light of the motel room.

"You're going to have to be quieter than that if you want to sneak up on me," Anton taunted, his voice dripping with malice as he pulled the knife tighter against Mia's delicate skin. " You must be asking yourself whether you can kill me before I kill her. Could you live with yourself if you're wrong?"

As Anton's demands grew more insistent, his voice taking on a manic edge, Hatch knew she was running out of time. Every second that ticked by brought them closer to a tragic end, and she refused to let that happen.

Hatch focused down the front sight of her gun, aligning it with her target. However, Mia's head obscured Anton's, making it impossible to get a clean shot without endangering the girl. Taking a lower point of aim would likely have dire consequences, as even a non-lethal wound could cause Anton to reflexively slash Mia's throat.

Hatch steadied her breath, the pad of her index finger pressing into the trigger and slowly withdrawing the slack, taking it to the breakpoint. She knew that the only way to ensure Mia's safety was to take Anton out with a single, precise shot between the eyes. But with Mia's head blocking her view, the margin for error was nonexistent.

Time seemed to slow down as Hatch weighed her options, her mind racing to find a solution. She couldn't risk taking the shot, not with Mia's life on the line. But she also couldn't allow Anton to continue this dangerous standoff, knowing that his instability could lead to a deadly outcome at any moment.

Hatch's eyes darted around the room, searching for anything that could give her an advantage. She knew she had to act fast, but she also needed to be smart. One wrong move, and Mia's blood would be on her hands.

With her heart pounding in her ears, Hatch made a split-second decision. She had to find a way to distract Anton, to create an opening that would allow her to take the shot without putting Mia at risk. It was a gamble, but it was the only chance they had.

Countless hours spent perfecting her marksmanship was brought into focus. A shot to the brain stem would cause instant incapacitation, preventing Anton from harming the girl even as an involuntary reflex. The margin of error was slim. The thin bone structure between the eyes left little room for deviation.

Hatch exhaled slowly, her sight oscillating in a holding pattern while she waited for the opportunity to present itself.

"Here's what's going to happen." Anton shifted, adjusting himself to further control the squirming child while maintaining the shield she provided. "I'm going to walk out of here. Your daughter will come with me for the ride. Once I get to my destination, I'll release her."

"You're not leaving with her." The gun trembled in Linden's hand. He spoke through gritted teeth. "It's me you want. I'm the one. Take me."

"How noble of you," Anton sneered. "But no. I think not. I like my plan better."

Hatch took a half step to the right, hoping to improve her angle. Still nothing. Anton must've sensed her effort as he took one step back.

"I'm losing my patience. You really don't want to see how this ends if that happens." Anton's voice was unnervingly calm. "So will you make another decision that costs *another* innocent girl her life? Or have you learned your lesson?"

Hatch watched from the corner of her eye as Linden began to lower his weapon.

"Wise choice. Now convince your friend to do the same."

Hatch heard Linden's whispered plea for her to lower the weapon. Deep down, her gut told her that doing so would surely seal Mia's fate. She'd come to listen to her gut and wasn't about to stop now.

Anton pressed the knife deeper. A small trickle of blood escaped the little girl's skin, rolling down her neck and disappearing beneath the collar of her Hello Kitty pajama top. Mia squealed. Hatch weighed her options.

Just as despair began to creep in, a shrill, buzzing sound cut through the tension like a knife. Hatch saw Anton's eyes flicker towards the source of the noise, his head turning a fraction of an inch. It was now or never.

In that split second, the world fell away, and Hatch's focus narrowed to a single point. Her breath stilled, her heartbeat steady, she squeezed the trigger with a smooth, deliberate motion. The gun bucked in her hand, the report echoing through the room like a thunderclap.

Time seemed to slow down as the projectile closed the distance to its target, covering the span of mere meters in the blink of an eye. The bullet found its mark, piercing the center of Anton's forehead, right between his eyes. The shot was precise, calculated, and lethal. The hollow-point round mushroomed upon impact, its energy rapidly dissipating within Anton's skull, causing catastrophic damage to his brain stem.

Anton's body went rigid, his knife clattering to the ground as his grip involuntarily loosened. His eyes, wide with surprise, stared blankly ahead, unseeing. In an instant, he crumpled to the ground, his lifeless form falling away from the little girl he had held captive just moments before.

Hatch maintained her aim for a split second longer, ensuring the threat had been neutralized. The standoff had been brought to an abrupt and decisive end.

The room swirled with motion as Linden rushed inside and swept his children into his arms. Hatch remained still, taking it all in. Her eyes scanned the room for the source of the rattle. Camila's arm trembled. She was holding the rattlesnake tail like a tiny maraca. Hatch walked over and gave her a hug. The girl sobbed against Hatch's shoulder for a few moments. She then untied her father.

"You saved our lives," Ernie said, choked with emotion.

"I couldn't have done it without your daughter's help. She provided a distraction that allowed me to do what was needed."

Linden continued to hold his children in a tight embrace. Hatch went to the Range Rover and retrieved a first aid kit from the trunk, then returned to survey Mia's injury. The cut to her neck was superficial. Hatch cleaned it with disinfectant. Mia took in sharp breaths at the sting of the solution. Then she placed a Band-Aid over it.

Linden escorted his children from the room. Ernie and his daughter followed. Hatch was the last to exit and closed the door to the macabre scene within.

"I don't know what the fallout from all this will be." Linden turned to Hatch. "Whatever it is, at least I can rest knowing that Anton Novik is no longer capable of hurting anyone else."

"You worry about taking care of your family. I'll take care of the rest."

"I don't know how to thank you."

"None needed. The world needs more people like you. People who don't stand idly by and let injustice go unserved. People who are willing to risk everything to protect good people and punish those who harm them." She extended her hand.

Hatch stepped away and placed a call to Jordan Tracy.

THIRTY-TWO

Chapter 32

As THE FIRST RAYS OF THE MORNING SUN CREPT THROUGH THE GAPS IN the curtains, Hatch stirred from her slumber. The events of the past twenty-four hours had taken their toll, both physically and emotionally, and she decided to skip her usual morning run. Her body had endured enough, and rest was now a priority.

She rose from the bed, her muscles aching with each movement, and began packing her belongings into her solitary military canvas duffle bag. The shirt she had rinsed and hung to dry after Camila's encounter with a rattlesnake still carried a faint red tinge, a reminder of the young girl's bravery and the chaos that had unfolded.

A knock at the door interrupted her thoughts. Hatch zipped up her bag and opened the door to find Banyan standing outside, his face etched with exhaustion but still managing a smile.

"Linden's already turned in his key," Banyan said, his voice gruff. "He'll be waiting for us in the Jeep."

Hatch nodded, glancing over at the room where Anton had met his end. Police tape fluttered in the breeze, torn and weathered, a remnant of the investigation that had taken place away from prying eyes.

"Tracy did a hell of a job clearing our tracks on this one," Hatch remarked, a hint of admiration in her voice.

Banyan grunted in agreement. "I don't know how, but he always finds a way."

Hatch tossed her duffle bag into the back of the Jeep and turned to face Banyan. "Meet you at the diner?"

"Sure thing," Banyan replied. "Linden will be there waiting for us."

With a nod, Hatch made her way to the motel office. As she stepped inside, she found Ernie behind the counter, his eyes blood-shot and his face lined with fatigue. In the corner, Camila sat at a table, lost in her drawing, her tiny hands moving with purpose.

Hatch approached the young girl and gently patted her head, a gesture of affection and gratitude. Camila looked up, her eyes wide and innocent, and offered a small smile. Hatch's gaze drifted to the stuffed rattlesnake on the shelf, its rattle now returned to its rightful place.

At the counter, Ernie looked up as Hatch approached. His eyes were filled with a mixture of relief and gratitude.

"I can't thank you enough for everything you've done," Ernie said, his voice thick with emotion. "Especially for saving Camila from that snake bite. I don't know what I would've done if..."

Hatch held up a hand, stopping him mid-sentence. "Camila is the real hero here. Her bravery saved the Linden family. She's the one who deserves all the credit."

Ernie nodded, a proud smile tugging at the corners of his mouth. "She's a special kid, that's for sure."

"That she is," Hatch agreed.

As she turned to leave, Ernie called out, "Where are you headed next?"

Hatch paused, a thoughtful expression on her face. "Wherever I'm needed, I suppose. There's always someone out there who could use a helping hand."

Camila's voice drifted from the corner, a soft melody of Spanish words. "*Que Dios te cuide y te proteja, así como tú nos cuidas y proteges a nosotros.*"

Hatch glanced at Ernie, a questioning look in her eyes.

"She's reciting part of a prayer," Ernie explained, his voice filled with reverence. "It roughly translates to 'May God watch over and protect you, just as you watch over and protect us.' I think it's her way of thanking you for all you've done."

Hatch felt a lump form in her throat, touched by the young girl's words. She nodded, a silent acknowledgment of the profound connection they had forged in such a short time.

With a final wave, Hatch stepped out of the office and into the bright morning sun. She climbed into the Jeep beside Banyan, her heart full and her mind at peace. As they pulled out of the parking lot and headed towards the diner, Hatch knew that whatever challenges lay ahead, she'd continued to be guided by the strength and resilience of those she had met along the way.

THIRTY-THREE

Chapter 33

THE COPPER CACTUS CAFÉ WAS BUSTLING WITH THE USUAL MORNING crowd. Hatch and Banyan sat opposite Linden and Carver. As they settled into the worn upholstery of the booth, the aroma of freshly brewed coffee and sizzling bacon filled the air, mingling with the scent of green chilies and spices. Hatch inhaled deeply, allowing the familiar smells to wash over her, a comforting reminder of the diner's charm.

Sue, the waitress from their previous visit, approached their table with a warm smile. "Well, look who's back! Good to see y'all again." She filled their mugs with steaming coffee before taking their orders.

Carver raised his cup. "Gotta hand it to y'all. Tracy said he was sending his best and he sure as hell didn't miss the mark." The Texan gave a shake of his head. "Never meant for it to go this route."

"Not your fault," Banyan chuckled, and thumbed in the direction of Hatch, "this one's a lightning rod for trouble."

"Guess trouble better look elsewhere." Carver gave a tip of his imaginary hat.

As they waited for their food, Linden leaned back in his seat, a look of relief on his face. "I gotta say, whoever you work for did a hell of a job clearing things up. The official story is that you two were undercover FBI agents working to stop an extortion attempt against me while simultaneously rescuing my family from Anton Novik's goons."

Hatch nodded, a small smile playing on her lips. "It's a clean story. Keeps your reputation intact and explains the shootout without raising too many questions."

"And I appreciate that the truth about how I framed Anton years ago never came to light," Linden added, his voice lowering. "I know it wasn't by the book, but sometimes you gotta bend the rules to make sure scum like him don't walk free."

Hatch met his gaze, understanding in her eyes. "Sometimes, the law isn't enough. We do what we have to do to ensure justice is served, even if it means crossing a few lines."

Banyan chuckled. "Just another day in the life of a couple of name-less, faceless heroes."

Sue returned with their plates, the tantalizing aromas making their stomachs growl. As she set down Hatch's omelet, Sue leaned in closer. "I just wanted to thank you again for the tip you left last time. It really helped me out of a tough spot."

Hatch smiled, recalling the conversation she had overheard thanks to Banyan's Omnisphere app. "I'm glad I could help, even if it was just a small gesture."

As they dug into their meals, the trio fell into a comfortable silence, each lost in their own thoughts. Hatch reflected on the events of the past few days, the close calls, and the lives they had saved. Moments like these, sitting in a cozy diner with friends and allies, made it all worthwhile.

Linden cleared his throat, drawing their attention. "I just wanted to say thank you, both of you, for everything you did. Putting your lives on the line to save my family and clear my name. I won't forget that."

Hatch reached across the table, giving his hand a gentle squeeze. "That's what we do, Linden. We look out for each other, no matter the cost."

As they finished their meals and prepared to go their separate ways, Hatch knew that the bonds they had forged through this ordeal would last a lifetime. In a world where the lines between right and wrong were often blurred, it was the connections they made and the lives they touched that truly mattered.

BANYAN CLIMBED INTO THE JEEP, settling into the driver's seat. As Hatch approached the vehicle, a thought crossed her mind. Now would be a good time to check in with her family, particularly Jed. She leaned into the open window of the Jeep. "Hey, Banyan, I'm going to make a quick call before we hit the road. I'll just be a moment."

"No worries," Banyan replied, nodding in understanding. "We've got plenty of road ahead between here and our next stop. I'll take the first leg."

Hatch stepped away from the Jeep and found a spot under the diner's awning, which provided limited shade from the warm desert sun. She scrolled through her contacts, finding Jed's number, and pressed the call button. After a few rings, a gruff voice answered.

"Well, if it isn't the world-saving hero herself," Jed chuckled, his voice sounding stronger than it had during their last conversation.

"Hey, Jed." Hatch smiled, relief washing over her at the sound of his voice. "I bet you're giving the hospital staff a run for their money."

"Damn right, I am. They've been poking and prodding me like a prized steer. I'm ready to get back to the ranch and breathe some fresh air."

Hatch leaned against the wall of the diner, watching as tumbleweeds danced across the dusty street. "I'm glad to hear you're doing better. I've been worried about you."

"No need to worry about me, kid. I'm too stubborn to let a little thing like a heart attack keep me down for long."

"I know, but I can't help but feel like I should be there with you and the family."

Jed's voice softened, a rare moment of vulnerability shining through. "Listen, Rachel, the world needs you more than we do right now. Your mom, the kids, they're all doing just fine. Jake and Daphne are growing up to be strong and independent, just like their aunt. And your mom, well, she's got me looking out for her."

Hatch felt a lump form in her throat, the weight of her responsibilities warring with her desire to be with her loved ones. "I just don't want to let anyone down."

"You could never let us down, Rachel. You're out there making a difference, keeping people safe. That's a noble calling, and we're all proud of you."

A tear slipped down Hatch's cheek, and she quickly wiped it away. "Thank you, Jed. I needed to hear that."

"Anytime, kid. Now, you focus on what you need to do. We'll be here when you're ready to come home."

"I will. And Jed?"

"Yeah?"

"Take care of yourself. I need you to stick around for a long time to come."

Jed chuckled, the sound warm and comforting. "Don't you worry about that. God and I have an agreement. I'll head upstairs when I'm good and ready. Plus, I don't think those angels are ready to deal with me yet."

"I'll hold you to that."

"You do that. Now, go save the world, Rachel. We'll be here cheering you on."

As the call ended, Hatch took a deep breath, her sense of purpose renewed. With Jed's words echoing in her mind, she squared her shoulders and walked over to Banyan's Jeep, ready to face whatever challenges lay ahead.

"Good to go?" Banyan asked as she entered.

"Always."

As the diner grew smaller in the rearview mirror, the vast desert stretched out before them, a landscape of endless possibilities and untold challenges. Hatch heard her father's words echo in her mind as they left the town of Diamondback behind. *Moving forward was the only way to keep the past from catching up.*

She remembered a moment from her childhood, sitting on the

porch steps with her father, his weathered face etched with concern. She had asked him, "What happens if the past does catch up?" He looked her square in the eyes, his gaze unwavering, and said, "You face it head on, kid. And never back down."

With those words ringing in her ears, Hatch scanned the winding road ahead, her resolve unwavering. She was ready to face whatever lay ahead, no matter the cost.

Rachel Hatch returns in *Redacted*.

https://ltryan.ink/redacted-release

Some Secrets Can't Be Erased

Hatch is tasked to provide personal security protection for a rising political star. His progressive visions garnering him the national spotlight have also made him a target and it's up to Hatch to ensure his safety during an upcoming campaign rally.

In the picturesque yet politically charged landscape of New Hampshire, an assassination goes awry. The shooter is on the run. Hatch joins the hunt. With every law enforcement agency hot on his trail, the walls are closing in.

As truths come to light, Hatch discovers an alternative narrative to the one she's been told. Knowing who to trust and what to believe is a matter of life and death. Her choice thrusts Hatch into a deadly game of deceit and betrayal, threatening to expose a sinister conspiracy, one people are willing to kill to keep silent.

The key to unveiling the dark secret rests in a rural community set in the White Mountains. As the enemy closes in, Hatch must put her trust in a man she barely knows. The stakes have never been higher.

Hatch is forced to put her code to the test. And the price of failure is death.

https://ltryan.ink/redacted-release

Join the LT Ryan reader family & receive a free copy of the Rachel Hatch story, *Fractured*. Click the link below to get started: https://ltryan.com/rachel-hatch-newsletter-signup-1

THE RACHEL HATCH SERIES

Drift

Downburst

Fever Burn

Smoke Signal

Firewalk

Whitewater

Aftershock

Whirlwind

Tsunami

Fastrope

Sidewinder

RACHEL HATCH SHORT STORIES

Fractured

Proving Ground

The Gauntlet

Join the LT Ryan reader family & receive a free copy of the Rachel Hatch story, Fractured. Click the link below to get started:

https://ltryan.com/rachel-hatch-newsletter-signup-1

Get your very own Rachel Hatch merchandise today! Click the link below to find coffee mugs, t-shirts, and even signed copies of your favorite L.T. Ryan thrillers! https://ltryan.ink/EvG_

ALSO BY L. T. RYAN

Find All of L.T. Ryan's Books on Amazon Today!

Deadline

End Game

Noble Ultimatum

Noble Legend

Noble Revenge

Never Look Back (Coming Soon)

Bear Logan Series

Ripple Effect

Blowback

Take Down

Deep State

Bear & Mandy Logan Series

Close to Home

Under the Surface

The Last Stop

Over the Edge

Between the Lies

Caught in the Web (Coming Soon)

Rachel Hatch Series

Drift

Downburst

Fever Burn

Smoke Signal

Firewalk

Whitewater

Aftershock

Whirlwind

Tsunami

Fastrope

Sidewinder

Mitch Tanner Series

The Depth of Darkness

Into The Darkness

Deliver Us From Darkness

Cassie Quinn Series

Path of Bones

Whisper of Bones

Symphony of Bones

Etched in Shadow

Concealed in Shadow

Betrayed in Shadow

Born from Ashes

Return to Ashes (Coming Soon)

Blake Brier Series

Unmasked

Unleashed

Uncharted

Drawpoint

Contrail

Detachment

Clear

Quarry (Coming Soon)

Dalton Savage Series

Savage Grounds

Scorched Earth

Cold Sky

The Frost Killer

Crimson Moon (Coming Soon)

Maddie Castle Series

The Handler

Tracking Justice

Hunting Grounds

Vanished Trails

Smoldering Lies (Coming Soon)

Affliction Z Series

Affliction Z: Patient Zero

Affliction Z: Abandoned Hope

Affliction Z: Descended in Blood

Affliction Z : Fractured Part 1

Affliction Z: Fractured Part 2 (Fall 2021)

ABOUT THE AUTHOR

L.T. Ryan is a *USA Today* and international bestselling author. The new age of publishing offered L.T. the opportunity to blend his passions for creating, marketing, and technology to reach audiences with his popular Jack Noble series.

Living in central Virginia with his wife, the youngest of his three daughters, and their three dogs, L.T. enjoys staring out his window at the trees and mountains while he should be writing, as well as reading, hiking, running, and playing with gadgets. See what he's up to at http://ltryan.com.

Social Medial Links:

- Facebook (L.T. Ryan): https://www.facebook.com/LTRyanAuthor

- Facebook (Jack Noble Page): https://www.facebook.com/JackNobleBooks/

- Twitter: https://twitter.com/LTRyanWrites

- Goodreads: http://www.goodreads.com/author/show/6151659.L_T_Ryan

Made in the USA
Columbia, SC
05 May 2024

35321187R00107